OH, MY DARLING

ALSO BY SHAENA LAMBERT

The Falling Woman
Radiance

OH, MY DARLING

STORIES

SHAENA LAMBERT

PATRICK CREAN EDITIONS
HarperCollins*Publishers*Ltd

A Patrick Crean Edition, published by HarperCollins Publishers Ltd

First edition

Some of these stories were previously published: "Oh, My Darling" in
The Walrus; "The Cage" in *Vancouver Review;* "The War Between the Men and
the Women" in *Ploughshares* and *Best Canadian Stories;* "Little Bird," as
"A Wandering Bird," in *The New Quarterly* and *Best Canadian Stories;*
"A Small Haunting" in *Zoetrope: All-Story* and *Best Canadian Stories;*
"Clams" in *Canadian Notes & Queries.*

The author acknowledges the assistance of the Canada Council for the Arts.

HarperCollins Publishers Ltd
2 Bloor Street East, 20th Floor
Toronto, Ontario, Canada
M4W 1A8

www.harpercollins.ca

Library and Archives Canada Cataloguing in Publication
information is available upon request

ISBN 978-1-44342-434-9

Printed and bound in Canada
DWF 9 8 7 6 5 4 3 2 1

For Madeline

CONTENTS

OH, MY DARLING

Hello, Vanessa.

Such a lovely name, with that sensual *V,* and those three satiny syllables. *Va-nes-sa.* There will be none of that diminutive stuff for me. No Nessa, or Ness, or, dear God, the worst of them all: Nessie. What on earth were you thinking, letting them call you that? It reminds me of the Loch Ness monster. I can just picture your size-fourteen body, mottled and walruslike, plunging into the sub-aqueous depth of that Scottish lake. Living your invisible life.

BUT wait. You must hear me out, I insist. Let's return to the day that everything changed for you. It was late February. February 25th, as a matter of fact. I remember the date. There were things to be done that morning and you did them. You were a genius at getting things done, taking care of your little family of three.

I can see you rising from the bed at 7 a.m., still full of sleep. Your satin nightie has slipped in the night. The breast cups face perilously eastward, full of nothing. While Callum slumbers on, you stumble to the bathroom, hitch up and take a pee, eyes closed, then plunge on with the morning. Next thing you are standing by the bed, shaking Callum awake. Your husband, blond and long-limbed, boyish even at forty-three, clutches at the quilt, wanting to block you out, and morning, and the bedroom.

The night before as he lay on the bed, Callum put aside his magazine to tell you he wanted to trace his family roots. You assumed he meant to Sweden or possibly, on his mother's side, to Scotland. You were tidying and turning off lights. When you glanced up, Callum had a blown-back look, as though he had stuck his head from a car window.

"Nessie," he said, "I think I have aboriginal blood in me."

Poor Vanessa. You stared at your blue-eyed husband. Even his underwear looked Scandinavian: soft flannel boxers in off-white. You raised an eyebrow, but your heart lurched. There you stood, solid as a tree trunk, with your hennaed hair and puckered arms, and you felt as though the floor had plummeted a dozen feet, like the deck of a boat. Callum is a partner in a law firm specializing in aboriginal treaty cases. His new articling student, Connie, is Haida, of the Eagle Clan. She looks it too, with her aristocratic nose and black eyebrows, hair falling to a slash at her chin line.

"What part do you think is aboriginal?" you said. "I hope it's something simple, like your foot."

And now you wake him. You poke at his languorous shoulder and tell him it's morning.

RAIN sheets the landing window as you come down the stairs to wake Aisla, your fifteen-year-old. The cedar tree outside looks wobbly and heavy. You can hear creaking as it throws its arms back and forth. But wait. A dream lingers in your head. You were high on a circus platform, wearing a sequinned leotard, and you were slim, the way you were in your twenties, hip bones jutting provocatively beneath the sequins. But (and this is the interesting part) for some reason the ringmaster was up there with you, dressed in top hat and tails. He was on a perch a dozen feet from yours, connected by a high wire.

Then all at once he danced across the wire and took your face in his hands. It was very Clark Gable, that gesture. But instead of kissing you, he produced a blue rubberized loop, like one of Callum's workout elastics, and with one deft movement he drew it over your head. There was such an ache in you, Vanessa, as you realized that he had danced so close, and tickled your chin with such intimacy, only to set you up to perform a trick—which was to step off the platform and spin by your neck in the air.

Now you pause on the landing, while downstairs the coffee machine comes to life on its own, chuffing and gurgling. Who was that man with his sensual, manicured fingers, and why was he placing a noose around your neck?

AISLA'S bedroom used to shine with prettiness, with its pony wallpaper, and the jewellery box with the ballet dancer that spun to *"Für Elise,"* and the wooden dollhouse. While Aisla went to swim class on Saturday mornings, you used to tidy her room, and then make the beds in that little house and set the tiny table. Now Aisla's floor is covered in towels, discarded clothes, dirty cereal bowls. The pony wallpaper is still there, but a few months ago Aisla circled the ponies with Magic Marker, then put question marks coming from their heads.

Aisla lies in bed, her short platinum hair sticking every which way, her face pure as a piece of crystal, though beneath her eyes the skin is faintly blue—the only hint that she returned home at two in the morning, on a school night, then showered for ages before throwing herself into bed. Worry sings in you, sings and sings. Briefly you imagine picking her up, carrying her to safety across a burning landscape. Instead you lean down and shake her awake.

"Fuck off," says the perfect mouth.

A pause. Then you pull the pillow out from under her head. Aisla sits up. She looks like an angry pixie.

"Fuck off, Mum, I'm sleeping."

"Don't you dare say 'fuck off' to me."

"Then don't come in and shake me."

"I was waking you."

"Okay. Fuck off. I'm awake."

You stare at Aisla. Aisla stares back.

"You're such a cow," says Aisla, and this hurts so much you draw in your breath.

"You are cruel."

"You are a fucking cow."

LET us pause here—mid-carnage as it were—to ask this question: *Why* does Aisla hate you so much?

Answer: because she doesn't. Answer: because she's afraid. Answer: because hormones are raging through her body like stray dogs, chewing out the inside of her brain. Because you are something solid she can bounce off. Because you are strong enough to take it. Because she took ecstasy three nights ago, and it is still doing a number on her small body's serotonin levels. Because she feels an inchoate hatred at the mere idea of you leaning over to shake her into wakefulness. When did her mother, her Nessa, whose lullaby voice sang her to sleep (a voice she equates with the moon), when did you transmogrify into this flesh-covered creature? What does this say about aging, about life? Because if she could, Aisla would hate you back into wholeness, all of her adolescent self gearing up for the task, because her job as a teenager is to refuse everything that stands in the way of a truth she doesn't even know she's clutching at.

So there you go. She hates you because she's refusing every concession you've made, and which you now wear in the form of moles and wrinkled gathers and creases cascading from the cleavage of your breasts. She is also (now that we are on the subject) refusing the wafting fat-lipped river of your twat, its Rio de Janeiro scent; the festival of grunts you make in the bathroom in the morning; and your giddy anger after three glasses of red wine, a dark voice waking in your chest, saying you, too, refuse to be this being that everyone takes you for.

But now we are back in the bedroom. And you are moving toward Aisla-of-the-many-hates, powering like a battleship across the detritus on the floor, and you are holding Aisla down, you have pinned her shoulders to the mattress while Aisla screams, *Get off me*, and you say, *Not till you say you're sorry*; and though Aisla is half your weight, she is fast as a cat, and she wrestles from your grasp and grabs your hair. *I can't stand you*, she is screaming. *I can't stand you.*

Then Callum is there, unravelling Aisla's fingers, and Aisla has broken from you and slammed the bedroom door so hard the wall mirror shakes and is about to fall. But it doesn't.

"At least she's up," quoth thou.

WHAT a morning. What an ordeal. With rope burns on your arms from Callum grabbing you, and your scalp tingling from Aisla's hair-pulling, you walk your golden Lab, Ginger, around the block. Rain sluices from your rain hat. The skin of your forearms prickles with suffering. All Callum said, as you left the bedroom, was, "That was unfortunate." And funny thing this: in the half-light of the window above the dryer, his hawkish nose and expressive cheekbones did look aboriginal.

You know he is thinking about Connie all the time now. Thinking about her taut and interesting butt, and about her grandmother, who showed her how to weave spruce root, the hands of the old woman beside the hands of the little girl. You have developed a clairvoyant sense, fine as a dog's hearing, for Callum's straying. Even now, watching him with such fear as he prepares to fall, this secret part of him appeals to you in an underground way, just as it seems to feed Callum—both of you fascinated by what this other Callum will do, the lengths he will go to. You know that when he leans close to Connie in court and breathes in the Herbal Essence in her hair, he may feel guilty, and ridiculous, but he also feels alive.

These thoughts gather in miserable clouds around your head. They drip along the seams of your hat. They run down your neck. But all the time I am so close. I am nearer, even, than the neighbour's oak leaf hydrangea, with its grizzled flower heads and peeling stems. I am so close you could touch me.

CALLUM bikes to work and Aisla buses (late again), while you drive, then park in the staff lot, facing the hedge with its yellow-spotted glossy leaves (such a depressing planting, chosen for indestructibility). The doors of Prince of Wales Elementary clank shut. Inside, you remove your hat and shake rain from your curls like a Portuguese Water Dog, then head down the hallway. Ah, at last. You open the door of your classroom, close it behind you—no wait, you lock it—and then zigzag between islands of Grade One desks to collapse in a beanbag chair, which sits on the carpet in this, the sanctuary you have dubbed Story World.

Yes, this is where you have been headed all morning: the incubating, productive hum of the school generator; the flicker of fluorescent light (you wanted to replace it with a standing lamp, for atmosphere, but the principal said no, it was a fire hazard); the spot of old blood where Kamal, your favourite, practised a pratfall and hit his head on a chair leg. Story World has a definite texture, from the wool-and-poly blend of the carpet, to the worn velveteen of the beanbag chair, to the fleece blankets you hand out. *Cover yourself in a piece of night sky,* you say, and the children do, tucking themselves into the serious job of imagining, of leaving earth.

Story World reminds you of listening, way back when, to Aisla playing dolls, after you tidied the dollhouse, the soft babble of pretending, so calming, like having your hair brushed. At moments like this you had an urge to write, didn't you. Sit on the carpet, pen in hand, and describe things. There's still an unrequited ache in your bones. I can feel it.

Lie back now. Garlands of red wool festoon the light fixture, and from these strands of Ariadne's thread hang the children's drawings of the Minotaur and the Gorgon, and the heroes too, Theseus and Perseus, some with blood dripping from their swords. You love to read myths and fairy tales, stories with dark centres. The children always perk up, lean forward. Why? Because something is at stake: death has entered the building. Though, recently a parent complained. They love what you do, inspiring the children and all that, but little David couldn't sleep in his own bed. You nod sagely, your whole body wagging with accommodation, but in your heart you will never surrender. Story World is your line in the sand, your Stalingrad, your Madrid—*¡No pasarán!*

Good for you, Vanessa. You'll need it.

THIS is the pattern of your day. The children rush in like a child-sea. They throw off boots or position them neatly, then take their places at their desks. You do roll call, and collect some forms, then hand out two dozen red foam noses. Kamal takes two and attaches them to the tips of his ears, which starts a trend. *Can I have another nose? Can I? Can I?* Then the children gather on the carpet. Dearest *Gott im Himmel*, how ironic. Today you choose something monster-free, a mouse that joins the circus, and of course it thrusts you immediately back to your dream, that rubber band pressing your vocal cords. But this mouse heroine is a multitalented little achiever (juggler, trapeze artist), though seriously underappreciated by the other performers. When the circus tent catches fire, it is she who leads the elephants to safety.

THE morning slides by. The morning grows fat and heavy. The morning disappears. You blink and you are in the staff room, with the smell of Miss Sugimoto's sandwich: tuna fish and brown bread and mayonnaise. You excuse yourself and go to the bathroom, close the metal door of the stall and fix the latch.

Vanessa, tell me this: Why do you do what you do next? Is it a gesture of theatrical grandiloquence, this placing of hand to breast? Or is it simply that you catch sight of yourself in the sheen of the bathroom door, and notice that two foam noses are still attached to the cartilage of your ears? You pull them off, then reach to place them on the metal sanitary box. This is when you feel a pressure under your arm, a rubbing on your bra seam. Odd. Now you reach inside your cotton blouse and press your breast beneath the underarm.

DEAR *Gott im Himmel.* Yes, Ness. This voice you hear, this combination of Humbert Humbert and Jack the Ripper, is coming from a five-centimetre invasive lobular carcinoma, ER-positive—a lump, in other words, cagily situated in your left breast, at two o'clock from the nipple. *C'est moi.* And if you please, I consider myself much too dark, much too personal to be described as a mere "lump." I prefer boutonniere of death. Or spider grafted to your flesh. Or *fleur du mal.* Invisible worm. Private monster. *Bête noire.*

The point is this, whatever you call me: I'm no lover you can stiff, Vanessa. Nor am I a loved one you can excuse, or observe with half-closed eyes over a brimming plate of dinner, senses bloated and lazy. No, my dear, let me make this clear. I will balance you on a razor. I will dance you across a rope so thin you will have vertigo. Don't look down. I will dress you in burgundy and sequins, I will call you the Cancer Queen, and my genius—for yes, I have genius—is that small and dark as I am (the size of a pea they think, at first, though they change that after the biopsy to the size of a walnut—STAGE THREE, Vanessa), yes, small and dark as I am, I suck everything into my orbit.

So here is my vow. There will be no dragon-boat racing for you, and no wearing of voluminous pink T-shirts. No throwing your arms around fellow survivors (careful, don't hurt that radiated shoulder)— no. This is my pledge. You will come out changed, skinned and clean, hip bones jutting through your leotard, having used every resource you have to fight me. (Witness, for instance, your eloquent but somewhat bizarre ministrations to this page. Here you sit, writing like the very dickens, attempting to expunge me from your system. Will it work? Perhaps it will. Remember that unrequited ache in your bones? Yes, perhaps it really will, coupled with tamoxifen, two surgeries, radiation, chemo, green tea and raw food.)

As for Callum, in the face of me (his moustachioed rival) he will snap to attention, his gallivanting falling away like an invisible garment. He will cover his face and weep when the doctor says the cancer has spread to the lymph nodes, and will weep again, in relief, when the doctor later says he believes that it has spread no farther. As for Connie, junior lawyer with a long and lovely nose, your high-wire act with mortality will simply blow her out of the picture, at least for now. And Aisla? One Saturday morning, after a particularly vomitous session in the bathroom, you will tell her you want a story, and she will run—actually run—to her room and bring back *Babar the Elephant,* and lie beside you in the bed, her fine, bird-down hair beside yours on the pillow. Yes, she reads to you, just as you read to her in bed when she was little, book balanced on your stomach so she could see the pictures. It turns out that what she really wants more than anything is for you to stay on the earth, large and dark, blocking the sun.

But wait. I run away with myself. I charge when I should pause and take in the moment. There you are, staring at two foam noses on a sanitary-disposal box, while the skin of your arms prickles and cools (the blood has fled your extremities to feed your beating heart). You see the knob on the door latch and, below that, a pattern of rust like a horse's head. Then you pull your bra back into place. You stand and flush and open the cubicle. Your face in the mirror—Oh, my darling! Your eyes. As though you know what is coming, what reserves it will take to flutter down from the ceiling and settle, with a terrible sigh, into your own body.

Beautiful Vanessa—allow me to dance forward and whisper these words in your startled ear: *Welcome home.*

THE CAGE

Manfred planned to lock himself in his cage again outside the Vancouver aquarium, to protest the captivity of dolphins and whales.

The cage, though barely tall enough for Manfred to stand up in, let alone lie down (he had to sleep curled in a fetal position), still managed to be terrifically difficult to load into the van. The side pieces were too long for the van's sliding door, and easing them in on a diagonal would never work because, as Leila, Manfred's wife of thirty-three years, pointed out, the side pieces were the exact same width as the top and bottom pieces, which had also failed to slide in on the diagonal.

"Last time we put them on the roof," Leila said. "Don't you remember?"

It was true. Last time, after a similar battle, they had tied all the pieces to the roof rack. But she knew there was no point now, in the midst of this Herculean struggle, explaining to Manfred not only that there was an easier way, but that they had discovered it years before. She went inside to watch the news.

Later, in bed, she felt Manfred roll in beside her, his bearlike body curving to hold her slight one.

"I tied them to the rack," he said. "You were right."

THE alarm rang at three in the morning. Leila made tea for the drive, pouring it into a Thermos. Manfred sat at the kitchen table, already in his jean jacket, staring at the backs of his hands, which rested on his knees. He had a handsome head of hair even now, thick salt-and-pepper curls that Leila had always loved to stroke. She thought he might have gone into a daze, but he looked up at her suddenly, brown eyes warm and awake.

"I was thinking," he said, "that we should be quiet so as not to wake Ilse. But of course she's not here."

Ilse, their grown-up daughter, lived on the North Shore now with a family of her own.

"I know." Leila nodded. "And how many years has it been?"

"Millions."

"Millions and millions. But we're still whispering."

THEY had done this twice before. The first time had been to protest the purchase of two dolphins from SeaWorld in San Diego. The second was because of Bella's baby, Chava. Bella was the beluga whale, and her birthing of Chava had been much heralded by the press and observed through glass by hundreds of schoolchildren. But after six days, Chava had died. Now Manfred was protesting the purchase of an orca from an aquarium in Nagoya. Kimalu had been caught off the coast of Iceland only three years before. It should, Manfred said, be reintroduced into the wild, not spend its days circling the tank, every now and then throwing itself into a back flip, getting fish handouts to cheers from the crowd.

So it wasn't new, Manfred's use of the cage. Still, Leila could feel the excitement building in him as they drove through the voluptuous, darkened city. He sat with his chest lifted, his face calm yet alert. She shifted gears as she pulled off Georgia Street and into Stanley Park. They followed the path of the seawall, past the statue of Percy Williams, a Vancouver boy who broke the 100-metre-dash record in 1929, now frozen forever, balancing on one heel, fists pumping furiously.

Manfred opened the window.

"Oh, don't," Leila said. "It's cold."

"I want to hear the tide." He gestured toward the seawall.

But the car was moving too swiftly for that, and in another moment Leila turned into the darkly treed parking lot of the aquarium.

None of this was new, but still, the *energy* as the car engine cut away. No other cars in the lot, thank God. Just the moon, pouring its fierce liquidity over the rocks marking the parking space, illuminating the metal buttons of Manfred's jean jacket.

Manfred unbound the bungee cords and untied the ropes.

"Stand on the other side."

For once they moved in sync. Manfred clambered onto the front of the van and lifted the top piece of the cage; Leila caught the other end and they lowered it onto the asphalt. Top, bottom, sides all came down silently.

They carried the pieces to the plaza in front of the aquarium doors. It took only a moment to decide where to set it up: close to the doors, but far enough from the fountain that, should it become windy, Manfred wouldn't get sprayed.

Nothing but the beam of the moon, the sound of the occasional screw falling on the polished granite.

They worked with such purity of zeal, Leila had to marvel. These moments were crucial: if they were stopped mid-set-up by a security attendant, the whole thing would come to nothing, and they would have to pack up and drive home, feeling ridiculous.

"There."

Leila paused on her knees, where she had been searching for a lost screw, and Manfred gestured to the cage, bungee cords in hand. Yes, there it was. Fully erected. Roughly the size of a refrigerator. Moonlight shot a shadowed grille across the granite plaza.

Leila sat on the lip of the fountain and poured out a cup of tea. Only a small sip for Manfred, or he would need to pee (he had a bottle for the purpose, but it was important not to over-hydrate). Out of solidarity, Leila took a smallish sip as well.

Then Manfred, with his beautiful curling head of hair and warm, brown eyes and clever, embracing palms and enormous convictions about the rights of whales and dolphins and animals in general, Manfred came to her and encircled her body in a hug. Then he stepped into the cage, swinging the door closed with a click, and Leila padlocked him in.

LEILA drove back along the Stanley Park Causeway, past the fountain shooting bright shafts of water high into the air. The forest was darker than the sky—you could see the tops of the trees. In another half-hour it would be dawn. Then it would be Leila's job to telephone the media, because Manfred refused to have a cell phone in the cage. She would read them Manfred's carefully worded press statement. Better to reach the assignment editors as they arrived at six or just after, rather than speak to a reporter on the night desk who wouldn't have the clout to break the story properly. That was Manfred's plan. After that, Leila would shop at the market, and then go home and cook lunches and dinners for the next week, things she could transport easily in heated thermal containers.

She imagined him as he must be right now, sitting in the cage, knees pulled up, wrapped in the brown blanket, his beard tucked under the edge. He would be alert to every sound. Then the dawn would come, illuminating what had been obscured: popcorn on the pink granite, a crust of bird shit on the edge of the fountain, popped remnants of balloons; and then at last, after what would feel like several days but was really only an hour, a car would pull up—the first of the media to have received Leila's call: Kim Kozak from *The Vancouver Sun*, or Morrie Chazen from *The Province*, or maybe, if they were lucky, an entire BCTV camera crew. And Manfred would stretch, already so stiff (it hurt his arthritis, these bouts in the cage), yes, he would stretch slowly, in that unhurried way of his, giving each leg a shake, and then, at last, he would deliver his words of compassion for the innocents: for Nakita, the resident orca, and for Bella and the dead Chava, and for the three dolphins, Kelsie, Wanda and Finn. And for Kimalu, who awaited transfer this very moment, in a concrete holding tank in Nagoya.

THEY had put the worst behind them: the difficult years when Manfred worked for Greenpeace and sometimes, for weeks on end, Leila didn't know exactly where he was—in the South Pacific or the North Atlantic, or the Arctic, chasing after Japanese whalers harpooning minke whales, or blockading nuclear-armed aircraft carriers. There was a framed photograph on top of the piano, which Ramona, their granddaughter, pointed to whenever she came over. It showed Grandpa driving a Zodiac, dressed head to foot in a yellow life-suit, beads of ice in his beard. It made Ramona laugh, and then their daughter, Ilse, would scoop the girl up and say, "Don't laugh, you little scallywag, can't you see that Grandpa is working really hard to save the animals?"

Manfred had been away for long periods. And then, when he was home, there had been *all that conviction,* which, let's face it, could get wearing over time. Why did Manfred have to care *so much?* Didn't he realize how hard it was for Leila at home, holding down a part-time job at the library, walking Ilse to school alone, eating dinner with Ilse, alone. She had been starved for adult companionship—a pervasive loneliness, which even now, years later, she could taste on the roof of her mouth; a feeling she had had at times, so hard to explain, that her skin, even, gave off a scent of deprivation, making people she might otherwise have been able to befriend (co-workers at the library, mothers in the playground) want to avoid her.

On Manfred's sea· voyages there were girls. Tough German girls and furious American girls and solid Swedish girls, all of whom called themselves women. They had hair on their legs, tufts of under-arm fur, and they went entirely without makeup. These were Manfred's colleagues: together they hung banners off buildings, slept suspended in the rigging of the Lions Gate Bridge, or wrapped them-selves in fish nets outside the Parliament Buildings in Ottawa, to protest deep-sea trawling.

Leila knew everything that had happened. Secrets would have debased their marriage. And through it all, their marriage was the most impor-tant thing, remaining constant when around them, to the left and to the right, their friends' relationships foundered in acrimony or ended in divorce. Still, campaigning had its own rhythm and logic, which wasn't all that easy to explain, though Manfred did struggle, many times, to do just that, telling her that together he and Leila could transcend the container of convention, with its restrictive and arbitrary rules. His argument was powerful. He loved Leila hugely: loved her slender body and freckled skin and blue eyes; loved the way she clipped her long straight hair into a bun, using a tortoiseshell pin; how she leaned close to Ilse, whispering, as though they had a secret language. There was nobody as important as Leila, he said—but surely she knew that? So shouldn't their marriage, grounded as it was in this knowledge, be capable of more than the stultifying norm? It seemed to Manfred that it should, and Leila, though she fought with him at first, found herself pulled like a dinghy in his wake.

What all this meant, in stark terms, was that Manfred, after he had hung a banner, or been chained for eight hours to a log boom, or narrowly escaped having his Zodiac torpedoed, went back to the mother ship, the *Rainbow Warrior,* and drank beer and ate vegetarian dhal, and there was Gretl, with her skinny arms, or Nancy, who hated her mother, or

Frieda, or Gudrun, or Sue—and of course he made love to them.

(Though Manfred confessed he spent much of the time, after the sex, talking about Leila—his love and her inhibitions, and what a wonderful mother she was. How he could never, ever, get along without her. His captive heart.)

"You could experiment too," he had offered, and Leila, making a sublime effort, had initiated a couple of trysts. She had no trouble attracting lovers, as it turned out. But the men had not interested her deeply, and the sex had felt awkward and useless. It was Manfred whose body she understood: the smell of his chest hair, the feel of his callused fingers. Even now, when all that other stuff was over, she still felt, driving along Denman Street, the city beginning to wake up, that Manfred, in his cage, was the centre, the exact centre, of her life. She imagined a Renaissance fresco with many figures, in town squares and on mountaintops, but always at the focal point of each motif was the prophetic, bearlike figure of her husband.

Driving the Zodiac.

Kissing her pregnant belly.

Taking Ilse into his arms for the first time. Weeping.

And now, standing alert and ready for what the

morning would bring: reporters, police, aquarium administrators.

Once, lying in bed, she had asked him to tell her the name of every girl. She wasn't sure why she wanted this. She was testing the limits of his truthfulness, perhaps, or her endurance. When he was done naming them, she had stared at the ceiling, picturing them not as people at all, not as girls or as women, but as an array of cunts: bushy red hair, black spare pelt, brown freckled lips—each vagina with its own scent, its own tautness and give. She had gone to the kitchen and made herself a peanut butter sandwich. As she stuck the knife into the jar she imagined being inside each girl, bearing down on her with an animal fury, pushing and forcing.

Even when Manfred had seen the light, as he did in his fiftieth year, and even when he had sworn a vow of faithfulness to her, and been faithful, now, for seven years, still those cunts persisted, floating dimly in the back of her mind. No longer potent. No longer capable of making her fling a peanut butter sandwich across a room. Just blowsy and unproductive, like flowers of the field.

She had made peace with them, she supposed as she turned under the Granville Bridge and headed toward the market. At last she had made peace with them. They could no longer harm her. Instead, they floated mutely at the back of her brain, like the sunspots of colour you get from gazing at a light bulb.

AT Granville Market, Leila got out of the van, stretched, then crossed to the square near the bread shop and sat on a bench. The main doors to the market had opened just minutes before. Already there was a bustle of vendors, trucks backing up and unloading boxes of cabbages, a florist setting out her bouquets beneath the corrugated awning. Now was the time for Leila to call the press, just as the first reporters arrived in their offices, poured their coffees, opened up their e-mails. She took out her cell phone. The numbers for *The Vancouver Sun* and the TV stations and the CBC radio newsroom were on her speed-dial. She was about to press the first button, when a bright commotion caught her eye. The three Ecuadorian men who so often played music in the square had just parked their pickup, and they were pulling a crinkly orange groundsheet from the back of the truck. She watched as they set up their equipment in front of the bakery, the man in the back handing down the drums first, and then the pipes and the synthesizer. Another fellow in a baseball cap ran an extension cord to a covered plug at the base of a pole.

Soon Leila would enter the marketplace. She would walk past the dazzling arrays of flowers, the buds of roses, velvet petals ready to unfold. She would pick out the food for the week, then go home and cook Manfred's favourites: goulash with egg noodles, moussaka and baklava, a lemon chiffon pie. At lunch she would beat her way past laughing schoolchildren and furious aquarium attendants to hand the thermal dishes to him through the bars of the cage.

"It's so delicious, Leila." That was what he always said. Grateful, abashed almost, by these hot offerings, after his hours of privation.

But for now the sun was about to touch the metal masts of the sailboats, torching them into flame, and all the masts were knocking together, making hollow tones like wind chimes. Seagulls cawed. And then, as though for her alone (vendors buzzed around her, but she was the only one sitting in the square), the Ecuadorian musicians began to play. Softly, tentatively, but then with gathering force, the air filled with the sound of their pipes, strange and ripe, a wordless song from a mountain pass Leila had never seen. And so she stayed exactly where she was, and listened.

THE WAR BETWEEN THE MEN
AND THE WOMEN

It is 1968, and there is a war between the men and the women. Jane hears it on the radio, where for the first time women's voices read the news; and she sees it at school, where her art teacher, Miss Hannah Shapiro, has started going bra-less, great wandering breasts shifting this way and that under soft denim; and there it is, on the bus: women travelling into Vancouver from the islands display gloms of hair beneath their arms.

At home things are still as a knife blade. Jane's father slices the ham, laying a piece on her plate, while her mother watches from her end of the table, wary and silent. Jane sits between them. She has the same foxy colouring as her father; the same sharp eyes and sandy lashes. She looks like a different race from her slender, bangled mother.

The curtains block out the back of Hollyburn Mountain. The neighbourhood dogs have been called in. Children are at their homework, or television, or sitting down to eat, though most eat earlier, and few follow such perverse rituals: multicourse meals with salad, ham and vegetables, dessert. Sometimes there is even a cheese plate, her father patting veined slabs of Roquefort onto English crackers. And there is wine, on weekends a half-glass poured for Jane. Even before things get bad, Jane feels like a chained dog, wanting to run around the table, wolf her food, bite someone's leg off. Anything to stop this nightly ordeal.

The overhead light casts its glow.

Her father's pointed chin is hidden but not forgotten beneath a trim beard. He wears a flannel shirt, over which he has donned a sweater-vest. He never wants to turn the heat up. As for her mother, doling out the scalloped potatoes, the only trace of her subversion is in the colour of her hands. Tonight her skin has turned crimson, with Prussian blue in the veins.

While Jane's father has been teaching at the university, her mother has been in the shed dying cloth, coating it with wax, cracking the wax to let the dye seep through, and then hanging lengths from the clothesline, where they drip ruby blood onto the grass. Then she has showered, changed, applied makeup, listening for the rev of Jane's father's MG up the driveway.

"Patrick," she says now, "how was your lecture on Hannibal?"

You can tell that he, Patrick Morris, has been waiting for this moment ever since getting home: just look at the need on his face. The martini and wine haven't hurt either, causing a slow emanation of dissatisfaction, like gas released from a chasm in the earth.

Yes, the students were the recipients of his annual lecture on the Second Punic War. No, they had not been inordinately impressed. They shuffled papers. They coughed. They asked the inane questions they always asked. He responded in Latin to flummox them, to make them feel the whip of his brain on their idiots' flesh. He told them that everything—*everything*—would be on the test, even the quotes he dropped in class, and that the tests themselves would come out of nowhere, like hailstorms.

"They have no conception of the challenges."

"I'm sure they don't." A murmur like a ripple in a stream.

Jane would like to put a fork through his head.

Tonight her mother, Gretchen, seems lighter than on other nights, less absorbed in the game, and Jane knows why. She has decided to enter one of her batiks in a juried craft show in North Vancouver. Now, as her mother nibbles the cheese-crusted potatoes, Jane can feel her mother carrying this knowledge like a bubble of mirth.

"It was merely the greatest ambush in military history," Jane's father continues. "Hannibal crossing the Alps, rising out of the mist, surprising Flaminius at Lago Trasimeno. But do these students care? Half of them are on acid. The other half want classes to be held on the beach."

Jane knows the story of Hannibal's ambush. Roman legions straggling along the shore at dawn, their lines dishevelled. All around them, the creaking of war wagons. The smell of fear in their horses' nostrils. Near the top of a far hill they could see the glow of Hannibal's campfires.

"Then Hannibal's men burst out of the forest behind them. Thirty thousand Romans caught without their armour, cut down where they stood. Three hours was all it took—a single morning. Tell me this is not amazing!"

(This is not amazing, Jane thinks.)

"The rivers turned red with the blood. They named towns after the bones and skeletons. Even today, farmers unearth collarbones, thigh bones, bits of armour."

Her mother looks up. Once upon a time she had a braid stretching all the way down to the small of her back, but now her hair is cut in a shag. The mole on her cheek is fingerprint-sized, and when Jane was little she liked to put her finger over it. Her eyes are deep brown, almost black, like the mouse pictured in Jane's old school reader. She smiles bountifully at them both, holding a piece of ham on her fork like a lollipop. "To me," she says, "it isn't actually about Hannibal at all. Or Scipio Africanus, or Flavius."

"Gaius Flaminius Nepos."

"The story–"

"It's not a *story.*"

"The history, then. It's not about the generals. Or even the dead—"

"Ossaia, Sanguineto, Caparossa, Pugnano."

"I see it all"—Jane's mother straightens her back—"from the elephants' perspective."

Jane laughs.

"Imagine"—her mother lowers her voice—"how shocked they must have been, coming from Africa, across the Mediterranean, shaken back and forth in the hold of a boat. Then up over the Alps, and what do they see? Snow!"

"They must have been freezing," says Jane.

"Nothing prepared them. Though perhaps an old elephant—some elephant guru two hundred years before—foretold the catastrophe, passing down the knowledge from elephant to elephant: 'A day will come, my children, when the sky will turn white and fall to earth in little pieces.'"

Her father watches his wife carefully. *"Ex Africa semper aliquid novi."*

"They must have gotten frostbite on their feet."

"Thirty thousand Romans caught without their armour."

"The skin of the elephants turned milky in the moonlight."

Jane's father pushes scalloped potatoes onto his upturned fork. A pea rolls away but is captured. "But why stop there, my love? Why not see it from the perspective of the camp dogs."

"Why not, indeed?"

"Or the cockroaches. Or the maggots. This is only the greatest military tragedy in history that you're ridiculing. In fact"—her father places his napkin by his plate—"you could be one of my students, Gretchen, because this is what I put up with all day." Before Jane's mother can speak again, Patrick stands. "The potatoes were over-salted," he says, "and you, my love, have had too much to drink." Then he is gone, to watch the television news downstairs.

Jane keeps her head down, examining her plate, which is stoneware with flecks across the surface like faraway birds. Her mother begins to clear the plates, pausing to press a crimson palm to Jane's forearm. Jane brushes it away. After a moment she hears her mother moving in the kitchen, ankle bracelet chiming like a lament.

JANE and her parents. They were conjoined like the Holy Trinity, but with her father always on top, interpreting the world for them, which was ridiculous, because Jane could clearly see that her mother, Gretchen, was the deeper one. When a hollow ache woke Jane at night, a fear of death that threatened to swallow her whole, only her mother knew the cure: she lay down, holding Jane's body with the length of her own, in her nightgown with its ribbon of apricot satin at the neckline, which left marks on Jane's cheek. Linked hands. Linked fingers. Said these words: *Life will feel very long.* And slowly, with the pressure of palm on palm, fingers enmeshed, smells—yeasty, earthy—rising from her skin and hair, her mother could make even the wild abyss of death disappear.

Gretchen also had subtler talents, which Jane did not wholly understand or respect.

After her father flounced from the table, Jane pushed back her chair and went into the kitchen. Why, Jane wanted to know, did her mother let him pronounce on everything that way? Why must the conversation *always* be about his work? And what about the elephants? Did her mother actually care about them—their hoary frozen toes, their terrible fate tumbling from Alpine cliffs, legs chained together—or was she just pretending?

"Why does this *always* happen?"

Her mother closed the refrigerator. Her eyes, meeting Jane's, were watery, humiliated, and for a moment Jane saw, really *saw*, that her mother did not have an answer.

"It's hard to understand when you're young."

"Yes, it is."

ONCE, when Jane was much younger, seven perhaps or eight, her father asked her (again this was at the dinner table) to name which of her parents she loved more. Later, when Jane was an adult, she wondered if this could even have happened. It felt less like a memory than like the fraught opening scene of a Greek tragedy, or a dream where everything spins calmly out of control. Jane remembered dancing around the table, grasping her mother's braid like a bell pull, and giving it a mean tug. When her mother threw her wineglass against the wall and ran to the bathroom, her father had shrugged sheepishly. "I think," he murmured, "we went too far."

Oh, they had made Jane complicit, an actor in their drama, the hair-puller! And that was what burnt. Even two decades later, when Jane was married, with a daughter of her own, and lived two thousand miles away, in Toronto, she remembered those scenes and she felt a burning in her throat, as though she were back there, held captive between them. It really shocked her, how out of control they had been, that was the truth of it: their lust for revenge, their parries and counter-thrusts, their sorrow.

Of course, she had to remind herself, it had been another age. Back in 1968 spontaneity had reigned. Women screamed and hurled china. Men got drunk and groped their students. Children threw themselves from the cliffs at Lighthouse Park, landing ramrod straight in the churning water. Everybody wanted things. Everybody asked and dug and jabbed and screamed—got stoned, got drunk: wanted.

But now the Age of Aquarius was over, and a new age had been ushered in: the Age of Boundaries. If Bruce, Jane's partner, felt the need to discuss their relationship, he arranged a meeting. He called her on the telephone, or told her over supper that he had things to discuss (and she did the same), and then they arranged a sitter for three-year-old Cara, and went to a coffee shop, or a wine bar, agendas in hand, and talked over their difficulties, carefully employing non-inflammatory language. Bruce was a scientist, a geologist. Once he caught hold of Jane's system of conflict resolution, he stuck to it with a rigour that verged, Jane occasionally thought, on the punitive.

Bruce's specialty as a geologist was the Niagara Escarpment. It seemed that some of the oldest trees in the world lived on the escarpment, holding on by their roots to pockets of soil compacted in the cliff walls. Some trees were over one thousand years old but only four feet tall. Some, the most gnarled and picturesque, were in danger from bonsai poachers.

Although Bruce, like Jane, worked for the University of Toronto, he headed out each morning wearing hiking boots and with a pack on his back, looking a bit like Charlie Brown (perhaps because of his round head, which made him look young, even in his late thirties). They were both, Jane and Bruce, ginger haired and blue eyed, a fact that embarrassed Jane. She hoped people didn't think they had chosen each other for that reason.

Jane was a historian in the Women's Studies Department. She focused on the Neolithic matriarchal societies (partnership models, she called them) of Anatolia and Thrace, which had been subjugated by waves of horsemen descending from the steppes: Kurgans (5,000 BCE), Ubaids (4,000 BCE), Hittites (2,000 BCE), Aryans (1,000 BCE). All these destroyers thundered down from the grasslands, brandishing swords and battle-axes, worshipping gods of the sky. Jane worked hard to make the terror real for her students. Imagine, she said, that you are out collecting shells, or bent over a well of indigo, and you feel the shaking of horses' hooves rising out of the ground. You run, but the chariots bear down on you with war cries and screaming, slicing of iron weapons; rape; dismemberment; your beloved son dragged behind a chariot by his hair. The Scythians, Jane told her class, attached pouches made of human faces to their reins, displaying them as trophies.

"How goes the war?" Bruce sometimes asked when she got home from work. Or: "How are things at the front?" This was a joke they shared, after coming across a volume of James Thurber sketches in a second-hand bookstore. The series, called "The War Between Men and Women," had really made them laugh. Line-drawn men with egg-shaped heads clubbed startled women with umbrellas. Gangs of dowagers retaliated by hurling canned goods down the aisles of the grocery store. Several women met in a lantern-lit barn to plan their next ambush. It was like the Second World

War—that was why it was funny. As though everything subverted between the sexes could be made public in the carnival of battle. Jane had photocopied the drawings and taped them to her office door, where they remained until a colleague mentioned pointedly that the cartoons didn't seem to validate women's struggle. Jane was up for tenure, so she took the drawings down.

Jane and Bruce worked at their relationship meticulously. They tried to be consistent. But still at night, sitting alone in the living room, while Bruce took his turn putting Cara to bed, Jane could feel the container of grief threatening to spill over. It wasn't anybody's fault. Certainly not Bruce's, with his open-hearted kindness, his ingenuity at fixing toasters and shower rods. And she and Bruce were both proud of what they had created, proud of their dispute-resolution mechanisms, their absolute equality.

I love you, he said as he left each morning, backpack on his back.

I love you too.

She suspected that he heard, as she did, the minute leap of faith required by this litany—as though they hoped, through repetition, to fan something wilder into flame.

———

BUT back in 1968 the evenings are all Sturm und Drang, and Jane lies in bed picturing the elephants. They follow Hannibal over the Alps, then down the body of Italy toward Gaius Flaminius, who is about to be severely outflanked. As Jane falls asleep, the two men, one dark, one light, take hold of each other and wrestle beside the lake. Hannibal's gold earring glints. Gaius is as skinny as a slice of moon. On they struggle, slick with oil, while behind them, with utter disregard, elephants chomp at the sweet lake-grass.

When Jane cries out, her mother is there, lying down beside her. To distract Jane, her mother sings songs, or recites the names of fishing flies she used to be able to tie, tricks her father taught her growing up on a remote lake in the Shuswaps, in the interior of the province, during the war. *Silhouetted damsels. Deer-haired nymphs. Goldenheads. Silver doctors.* These names cause a ruckus and shine in Jane's head. She lies beside her mother, picturing the hunting and fishing lodge with its cookhouse, and eight wooden cabins with green shutters that can be raised and lowered on hinges. Wood stoves for heat. Four outhouses.

It wasn't a camp people brought their children to. There were just men up from the city on hunting trips, or expert fishermen or, now and then, a couple, like the honeymoon couple who came thinking the place would be romantic. The lady, bored and fretful, tried to suntan at the end of the dock, which turned out to be impossible because of the bugs. The day before she left she painted all of Gretchen's toenails red.

It is her mother's loneliness that Jane feels, each time she hears the stories. Jane closes her eyes, and she can see her as a little girl running after her father through the long grass, and this image radiates a great throb of loneliness from its centre.

She sees her grandfather Hans pulling on his work boots, and then walking past the cabins to stand on the dock. Gretchen runs after him and slips without a word into the bow of the rowboat. She feels the thunk of the oar blade against the dock as they push away, shooting across the reeds. They row past Butterfly Cove and Mermaid Rock, toward the dark side of the lake. Hans casts and trout come to his hook, but Gretchen, aged five, doesn't care about the fish anymore.

"How many days?"

First it is one hundred sixteen. Then eighty-three. Then—miraculously—sixteen. Sixteen days until the end of banishment. Sixteen days until the first day of school.

Gretchen sees her father looking toward the end of the lake where the outlier cabin sits in its private cove. One of its shutters is off-kilter. He rows into

the bay, ties up to a sapling, and they go to investi-
gate. If a wolverine has been inside, it could have
done serious damage. Wolverines are ferocious and
carry long grudges. Gretchen can feel her father's
worry. He pulls open the door, and mattress ticking
floats everywhere. The bed has been knifed open,
canisters overturned, bacon grease and cornmeal
spread on the floor to form a messy swastika. And
the worst part—someone has taken a shit on an
enamel plate and left it on the card table.

As for the first day of school at Sicamous
Elementary—it was inevitable—how could it not
be? This little girl from the woods was bound for
sorrow, just like a character in one of the folk songs
Gretchen sang. No friends were going to gather
around her in pastel dresses, bows in their hair: not
likely. She was an enemy alien with scabbed knees
and a German name, whose jacket smelled of woodsmoke, whose parents couldn't afford saddle shoes.
What happened next was as inevitable as coughing,
as lying down, as dying—and Jane wishes, whenever
she hears the story, that she could go back in time,
step from behind a corner of the schoolhouse, walk
past the tittering girls and take her mother's hand.
I'll play with you, is what she would say, if she had
that kind of power.

———

BUT now it is 1968, and the women of West Vancouver are swollen with different longings. They tie-dye their husbands' handkerchiefs while they are at work; they use the good silver to hot-knife hash; or, like Jane's mother, they spread moon-like silk on the table in the woodshed, and prepare to make something beautiful, while in a nearby cedar a woodpecker goes at the bark with hydraulic force.

On this day in April all the tulips open at once, showing their stamens like dog penises. Jane walks home from school at lunchtime. She doesn't like to eat in the playground because some of the boys have named her Gorki Pickle. Now why have they done this? Is it her plump stomach? Red hair? White legs? Boys seem to sense the changes in her body: breast buds, softening nipples, the arrival of foxy hair around her pubis. She smells of sabotage.

To make matters worse, Miss Shapiro, her favourite teacher, has told the class she plans to leave school mid-term, right after Easter break, in order to travel to Mexico. She uses the term *find herself*— she wants to *find herself* in Mexico—inspiring Jane with the cloudy understanding that one's self can actually go missing. And suppose (this was what her father said later, when he heard)—*suppose* Miss Shapiro were to go to Acapulco, but her self was in Puerto Vallarta.

Jane opens the back gate, salami sandwich in one hand. The yard smells of wood bugs and mulch, a leafy scent of decay. The shed door is open and her mother is singing. She has a good voice, mellow and low, and Jane, stepping along the gravel path, feels the song like a caress. The boys' teasing and name-calling dissipates in the cedar-filled air.

Inside the shed, Jane's mother stands over a table covered by a length of white silk held along each edge with carpenter's clamps. It is taut as the skin of a drum and has a bluish cast to it. She has a tjanting in her hand—a penlike instrument with a fluted spout, out of which she can pour a line of wax. The fabric reflects light onto her cheeks and forehead.

"You're home. Everything okay?"

Jane nods. She cannot say to her mother, *They call me Gorki Pickle.* She cannot say, *I am crushed by something large on my chest.* Jane reaches out a finger to touch the fabric.

"Are your hands clean? It's watered silk."

Watered silk.

"It's slippery," Jane says.

"I was just about to make my first mark."

It is almost too exciting, this immortal moment, with its honey scent of beeswax and paraffin, the enamel pot bubbling on the hot plate, ready for the poisons—acid blue, mordant yellow, raw sienna. Her mother cups her hand beneath the tjanting and stares down at the pure swath of fabric. She cocks her head, narrows her eyes, and something artful in this birdlike gesture makes Jane wince. Gretchen shifts her weight, preparing to touch wax to cloth, and she seems all at once like a puppet, falsely radiant with the effort of making this one moment matter. What does she hope for? Jane feels an itch of irritation gather under her clothes. Only much later, as a grown-up, does she understand what her mother must have needed. She wanted a ripe line of wax to flow from the tjanting, such as might come from the pen of a Zen calligrapher: thick, thin, even, uneven, pure, followed by another, and then another; moments of grace: God visiting her softly, without fuss, right there in the backyard woodshed.

That was all.

BACK at school, Miss Shapiro has gone to the principal, telling him that she intends to leave at Easter break.

"You can't," he says.

"I have to."

"Then go now. Right now." The gauntlet thrown.

When Jane enters the art room after lunch, Miss Shapiro is kneeling in front of the supply cupboard, a clutch of her favourite girls around her. She is telling them that authority does not always understand the dictates of the heart. At the same time, she is separating construction paper into two piles, as some of it is hers.

One of the girls says, "Gorki Pickle, go away."

But Miss Shapiro says, "Don't be ridiculous. Jane, you come and help me."

And Jane stands with a skein of wool around her forearms while Miss Shapiro winds it into a ball.

By three o'clock Miss Shapiro is gone.

Outside the sky has turned a darker blue. At the edge of the school parking lot boys are throwing each other into a juniper bush, calling each other *homo*, which allows Jane to slip by. Night hovers in the distance, hours away still, but Jane begins to hurry, kicking a pebble with the arch of her left foot and then her right, making sure that the stone touches her shoe seam each time. A limousine is parked in the church lot, and Jane feels a wash of terror remembering the rhyme:

> *If you should see a hearse go by*
> *Then you will be the next to die.*

But there is nothing to be alarmed about.

Hurry. Kick the pebble. Hurry. Wait. She passes her

Italian neighbour's place, with its chicken coop, then the bramble-covered vacant lot, the big rock at the corner sprayed with the words *Fuck the dogs.* On she goes, up the driveway. She doesn't realize yet how easy it will be to escape; that one day a solution will arrive, along with long legs, training, marathons— the secret being simply to keep moving, to outrun them. For now, all she can do is take hold of the front doorknob, push the door open, and then call out once.

Jane's mother fumbles with the bedroom door, then floats down the hallway. She plants a kiss on Jane's cheek with burning lips.

"How was your day?" The spark in her mother's eyes has been snuffed, and her hair is a static mess, as though brushing had confused her and she'd stopped halfway through. And yet her half-smile as she asks this question is sly. Yes it is. Slyly gleeful at having escaped them. Like Miss Shapiro she has fled, leaving only this sepulchral, loose-haired, vod-ka-imbibing presence.

"I'm calling Dad," Jane spits at her mother.

"No, don't. Please don't." Gretchen sits down heavily on the bottom stair and begins to weep.

Jane turns to stare at her. How can this happen? (And happen so often—each time taking Jane completely by surprise.) How can her mother—Gretchen the Lonely—Gretchen the Beautiful—turn into this weeping troll at the bottom of the stairs?

What makes oblivion so worth it?

1968. Gretchen showers noisily, banging against the shower stall. Then she comes upstairs in a clean, floor-length caftan. She sits in her chair by the fireplace, hotly washed and scrubbed, as though for sacrifice.

At last Jane hears her father's MG rev up the driveway. His car door slams, his key scratches the front door latch, his briefcase makes a muffled thud on the parquet floor.

From her place in the kitchen, Jane can see both her father grimly mounting the stairs, and her mother sitting with her ankles crossed, staring at the charred bits of log in the fireplace. Her father crosses the rug to stand in front of her. He shakes his head, a jitter, almost a tic.

He says, "Please, Gretchen."

"I'm sorry," she whispers.

"No." He shakes his head again, his face reddens, and he sits on the hearth stone. Then, as though that were not far enough, he slides to his knees and places his face in her lap. There is no sound, except for the refrigerator, which whirrs and stills. The part in his hair has turned pink.

Gretchen looks out at him from the vast field of her loneliness (she is crossing a moor at twilight, she is alone), and then she reaches down to stroke the back of his head.

CROW RIDE

Muriel was given the leaflet at Whole Foods. Not inside the doors, where Swiss chard was mounded high in a Christmas display. Outside. Beside the peonies from Chile, a dollar a stem.

A young man with dreadlocked hair danced toward her. His hands, yellow from grime (or was it natural dye?), contrasted sharply with the sleeves of his woollen sweater. He produced a flyer from his satchel, flicked it inside her comfort zone, and flashed her a smile.

Surprisingly bright teeth.

"Crow ride?"

Muriel tried to sidestep him, but he boxed her in against the peonies, blood maroon and seashell pink. They must have travelled on ice for thousands of miles only to land in this cold harbour, this rain-forest mist. Up close the man smelled of the brine in feta cheese. How old was he? Twenty. Twenty-two at most.

She said, "I don't know what that means."

Again that grin. He pointed to the flyer. "We bike to where all the crows roost at sunset."

She asked him where they roosted and he gestured east. At Still Creek, he said. Beyond the outskirts of Vancouver, in Burnaby. Costco had built a big-box store there, so this group—the crow-riders—was protesting. He had a sharp, almost goatlike chin, and a fleshy mouth, and surprisingly clear, interested eyes, though she suspected that he had contempt for them all—all the middle-aged Whole Foods shoppers. She had an urge to reach out and touch one of his dirty-blond dreads with the pads of her fingertips. They were frowzy and inviting, like strands of rope.

"You should come."

"Crow ride." She sounded the words, and then gave him a bright, false smile she regretted instantly. "I'll think about it."

MURIEL went from cooler to shelf, placing mandarin oranges and sugar and flour in her buggy. She would bake cookies for Arabella, her twelve-year-old daughter, and for Pan, her husband, leaving them on a plate on the counter, an offering of Christmas cheer. Pan would come home from work, shower away the fine gold dust from the construction site, then grab a cookie and drive Arabella to dance class. She—Muriel—would be at her step class and when she got home, Pan would already be in the basement, working with his lathe.

Muriel caught a glimpse of herself in the mirror above the spinach. Medium-length hair and that kind of thin, sad face you see on older women. She hoped that the boy wouldn't be there when she left the store, to see her paper bags so stuffed (she had forgotten her cloth ones). When she came out, he was gone.

It was only when she was in the kitchen unpacking the groceries and something black shook the phone wire outside the window—a squirrel—that the words *crow ride* formed again in her mind. She went to the computer and Googled "crows":

Crow flights
Crow intelligence
Crow ride

A picture of bare-limbed trees. She clicked "enlarge," and black flecks darkened the sky. *Still Creek at Dusk*, the caption said. At first glance the trees looked cankered, but these knobs, on branch tips and tree crotches, on every limb and joint, were, in fact, the roosting crows.

Muriel put some ground turkey on to fry, then stood with the wooden spoon in her hand considering her granite counters. They had been constructed to ward off dread. But dread had arrived anyway. Perhaps she and Pan had even coaxed it into being by installing such solid, immaculate countertops, and the pullout drawer for spices, and the two nooks— computer and breakfast. This kitchen had been their dream, and God had smote them for it. One of the things God was good at: smiting you for getting your priorities wrong, for basking in the glow of maple-stained floors, faucets that didn't drip, the look of a stainless-steel bowl holding three Anjou pears.

Their teenage son, Alexander, had died of a drug overdose while they were finishing the base-boards—Pan thinning the shellac to brush the wood with its third and final coat.

THAT night she dreamt Alexander was sitting on the blanket box at the end of the upstairs hallway. She came toward him tentatively, floorboards creaking under her feet. Behind him the window was open, and she realized this was how he must have gotten in. His fine dark hair, which showed the bones of his head, stuck up as though pulled by a static comb.

She knelt to look into his eyes. He met her gaze with a kind of watchful compassion, as though he saw right into her, but it was up to her, now, how things would go.

You're back, she whispered.

Don't tell Dad.

He crossed his legs, then picked a speck of tobacco from his teeth and flicked it away. Where had he been? Under the ground? In some dark place? His acid-washed jeans smelled fermented, vinegar-like. They would have to be cleaned, that was what she thought next, and that brought other thoughts, even as she knelt in front of him: how they could have a proper Christmas now. Morgan would come back from university, and all three children would tumble down the stairs on Christmas morning and sit by the tree. Even as she composed this picture she felt a streak of misgiving, and when she glanced back at Alexander, silver coins covered his eyes. They were the size of dimes, but ancient, the imprint rubbed from them as though they'd been run over by a train. Muriel cried out and tried to peel one away, but the coin was attached, and tearing at it seemed to be leaving a hole in his iris. *You have to take your Adderall,* she kept saying. *You have to take it, Alex. If you don't, this happens.* But Alex didn't seem to care whether he could see or not. He rocked back and forth, moving his head to the heavy rock coming from his earphones, smiling inside his blindness.

THE next afternoon, around three o'clock, Muriel put her bike on the car and returned to the store. The boy was there, though the peonies were gone, replaced by buckets of twiggy branches covered in berries. His sweater was heavy with raindrops. A Rasta hat covered his dreads.

She said, "I'd like to go on the crow ride."

He met her eyes. He didn't seem as nice as the day before; perhaps the rain was getting to him. He said, "It only happens once a month." Today he was giving out flyers for an arts cooperative. Hand-stitched pillows.

Who pays you to do this? she wanted to ask, but instead she apologized; she had thought the crow ride happened every night. "Maybe I'll come next month," she said. The doors opened, releasing her into the spruce-scented store.

She was picking out cheeses, her hand on a Saran-wrapped triangle of Port Salut, when she smelled him behind her, hops and sweat. "Oh!" She wheeled around. "We meet again."

He had appeared so suddenly, she thought he might be about to hurt her; but instead he smiled gently, then placed his yellowed palm over her hand—the one grasping the bar of the buggy—and closed his eyelids. There they stood, swaying slightly, she with the cheese in her hand, drenched with embarrassment at this New Age silliness, he with his long nose, chiselled lips, prominent freckled cheekbones.

Then he opened his eyes and winked. Or did he? It was so quick she wasn't sure she'd seen right. It was as though he, too, couldn't quite believe the schlocky gesture.

"I can take you there," he said. "Still Creek."

"Now why would you do that?"

"You should see them for yourself."

Above the coolers, in the ventilation system, she heard a bat-squeak of warning. She looked carefully into his eyes, and he nodded slightly, returning her gaze, as though to say, *I know what you want.*

"Besides," he added, "you seem like a nice person. You have a car, right?"

• • •

THE trees of December were shorn of their leaves, great limbs brushing the sky. Muriel turned onto Fourth Avenue and they drove past lululemon, travel stores, a Thai fusion restaurant. All this had once been a hippy strip—varnished counters and stained glass, organic cheese and manna breads. That era was gone, and all that was left was this boy, transported here in his hippy garb.

Muriel noticed that the rain had stopped. All at once a streetlight flicked on, followed by another and then another, all down Fourth Avenue. There was only an hour of light left in the sky. In ten days it would be the shortest day of the year. And then what?

"Just keep heading east."

"On Fourth?"

"Why not?"

He turned and gave her that smile, and again she had the sense of being exposed, as by a camera flash. She pictured herself from his point of view—her tucked-in blouse and high-waisted jeans, her neatly combed hair and horsey face. She had put her ski jacket in the back seat, and now she wished she had its protective covering.

"Did you go to high school around here?"

"I'm travelling, actually. I'm a travelling man." He began to tap his index fingers against his legs, then noticed and stopped.

"Where are you from?"

"Back east. Peterborough."

They were moving faster now, through a district that had once been warehouses but was now all cream concrete and aqua glass condominiums. She asked what he was doing in Vancouver and he said he had been going to university, but he'd dropped out after a semester and now things were much clearer.

"I'm liberated," he said. "But also hungry."

Muriel pictured an exasperated father. A doting, worried mother.

"So you make money by giving out those flyers."

"I work for a business that charities hire." Most of the charities were big, like Oxfam or Red Cross, but he and some of the other canvassers gave out pamphlets for local groups too. Like Crow Ride. It was all legit, he said, though it didn't pay much. He beat a rhythm on the thigh of his jeans. Hit the cymbals. "And I steal things."

At first she thought she hadn't heard right: he said it the way someone else might say, *And I have a paper route.*

"Where do you steal from?"

He shrugged. "Whole Foods. 7-Eleven. And then you can always scrounge from the dumpsters. Did you know the curry house on Commercial Drive gives away all their curry at the end of the day?"

There was a pause as this information sank in.

"You look sad," he said. "Am I making you sad?"

She shook her head.

The Science Centre glittered in the afternoon mist like a Christmas bauble. The boy crossed his legs and began to pick at a hole in the thigh of his jeans. She caught a glimpse of faded pink long underwear. He reached forward, fingering the dial of the radio.

"Can we?"

"Sure."

He found the classic-rock station with no trouble and Mick Jagger filled the car, singing the words *star fucker* over and over.

The boy leaned back, ankle on knee, foot waving to the music. A host of tics and buzzes emanated from his body. Did he do drugs? Yes, he probably did, and she realized she had known this already. There was a type, and he was it. He was also clearly used to being driven around by a mother.

She said, "My son died of a drug overdose" at the same time that the young man said, "I just need to make one stop."

They let each other's statements sink in.

"I'm sorry, man," he said. "That's rough."

"Where would you like to stop?"

"It's pretty much on the way."

"Just say where."

"You can turn here."

She executed a left turn on Main Street.

"This will only take a second."

He had been couch-surfing at his friend Zoe's house, he said. But the sad truth was he had to pick his stuff up by the end of the day or she was going to throw it in the dumpster. "She has a hate-on for me right now." This was because he had slept with her friend Maggie. Maggie and he had just had this *thing*, this dynamism. It was impossible to resist. And now Zoe was screaming at him all the time. "Fuck."

"Sounds difficult."

"It's like I have this jagged piece of glass stuck right here." He touched his chest.

There was silence.

"And all I want to do is travel to Baja. I have this idea I could skateboard to Baja—I'd be the first person in the world to do it. I've heard the light down there is really different." Full stop.

Slowly his mind seemed to circle around to her again. "I'm sorry about your son," he said.

She shook her head. Too late, selfish boy. Too late.

"It's just"—he tucked one foot under his thigh and turned to look straight at her—"it's out of my experience, even to *have* a son. And when something is way out of my experience I get distanced. I'm sorry."

She nodded tersely.

"I feel this prickly confusion all over me. And it's like I'm a thousand miles up and I'm staring at the world. And then I think, just as it becomes fucking unbearable, maybe I'm enlightened, maybe this is what enlightenment is, seeing everything from on top, you know, and from a huge distance." There was a pause, and then he added, "Or maybe I'm just an asshole. You turn at the next right."

This last was so transactional, her anger must have registered on her face.

"Don't look at me that way," he said.

"Where do you want to go?"

"Tell me about him."

Nothing.

"I shouldn't have said that, about being distanced. I was trying to be honest, but sometimes honesty—"

"I just want to see the crows and get back by dinner."

They slipped under the viaduct and into Chinatown. They were closer to the port now, the sea almost washing under them. They passed the Ga Cheong Herbal Medicine Company, bins mounded with iridescent fish slivers. A golden cat waved its arm up and down. *Hello and welcome,* it said. *Hello and welcome.*

"What drug?" he asked gently.

Despite her anger, she heard herself say the word, *ecstasy.* Always so full of promise, that name. It was a mix of drugs, actually—E, ketamine, OxyContin, plus his own medication—but she didn't want to give the boy any more than this.

He sat with his hands palms upward, back straight, breathing deeply, as though calming himself against the onslaught of something: the onslaught of her, no doubt, and all the unwanted stuff she had opened in him, about distance and compassion—and death. Again she smelled that odour he emitted: hops and cheese and something deeper and riper, like truffle oil. She said, "This isn't a particularly great way to get to Burnaby."

They were in the heart of the Downtown Eastside now. They drove quickly past a skinny prostitute with caved-in cheeks, a condition, she happened to know, that was caused by grinding your teeth. Caused, in turn, by crystal meth. At the corner of Main and Hastings, another prostitute veered up to rap on the window, then saw Muriel and turned away, muttering.

The boy laid a hand on Muriel's thigh. "I am very sorry about your son," he said. "I am, you know. I really am."

NOW they were pulled over in front of a dilapidated pink house on Heatley Street, and Muriel was crying. She was crying because this boy had such wise eyes. His words were stupid. His gestures were stupid, but his eyes were very kind. She cried because of her dream, which kept coming back to her in fragments, and because Alex was her second child, and because it had been so long since a boy had flicked the radio on beside her, or bobbed his head to classic rock, or rested his runner on the glove compartment.

She wiped her eyes and stared out at a hydrangea bush with sepia pom-poms.

"Tell me," the boy said gently. Where had he learned to be so kind?

She told him bits and pieces from her storehouse of grief. How they had listened to the doctor, who had prescribed medication. And how when Alex was fifteen, experimental child that he was, he started snorting that medication with his friends. How within a year Muriel and Pan were locking Alex out of the house because he was dealing in all kinds of drugs—E, K, M (an alphabet of terror)—buying, selling, railing, snorting it—and stealing things from them to support his habit, like an entire stereo system, and Pan's stamp collection. How one night Alex had tried all the windows, and then leapt down from the roof, breaking the stems of the rose bushes, and run down the broad boulevard to meet friends at the beach, where, in a clearing in the bramble patch, he had taken a heroic dose of mixed drugs and floated out of his body. How he had said to his friends, before he lost consciousness, that he could see every bunny in the patch. She always pictured him, when she relived this, as floating at tree level, lit up with milky brightness, like the moon.

There was more underneath, too, that she didn't say, but which the boy seemed to understand: that their first child, Morgan, had been so easy, and their third child, Arabella, had been easy; but their second child, the one everyone said was supposed to feel small and sandwiched, he had cried for hours as a baby, and he wouldn't take the nipple, and as a toddler if you gave him a toy car to play with, he drove it up your leg. It was never enough that he should have fun; he had to bother you. He radiated darkness, that was what she had felt at times. He was called by other gods. He had *disorders*, that was what the doctor said. And in the end it was a relief to classify what was going on, to say, *He is a boy with disorders.* But she will never forgive Pan for agreeing so readily to the medication. And someday soon she will leave Pan, and perhaps this is the first stage (she doesn't say this, but the boy understands). She wants this to be the first step into another land, though in fact she knows Pan is not to blame. It is just that Pan never rose fully to the occasion, he wasn't present enough, he didn't pay attention; and neither did she, not really, not fully. They both had Attention Deficit Disorder. And now Pan wants things to be normal, if they can be. They even have a plan to take

Arabella to Europe this summer. But none of them know yet that there will be no Europe. She will blast them to pieces. She will burn their fields.

This was what she didn't tell the boy, but what he understood anyway.

He said, "Come here. Let me hug you." (Oh God! The corniness!) But she turned to him and let herself relax into his woollen arms, and to her astonishment she felt at home. It was as if she were sixteen again, being embraced by a boy in a car. And to her further astonishment, she felt his lips on her hair.

He said, "You're beautiful. You really are. Do you know that?"

And she wanted to say, *No.* She wanted to say, *I should be killed. I locked my own son out of the house. I heard him rattle the window.* Instead she sat up, got a Kleenex pack from the glove compartment, and blew her nose.

"Go and get your things," she said.

"You are a beautiful human being."

He got out and loped to the concrete stairs leading to the house, then he turned and came back and knocked on her window. When she unrolled it, he leaned in, stroked her cheek, and kissed her tenderly near the corner of her eye. A sizzle of electricity leapt from his lips to her skin.

"You never told me your name. Mine's Simon."

She heard herself say her name. Then the boy—
Simon—turned and took the concrete stairs two at
a time, giving the stone lion by the gate a friendly
tap on the head.

ONCE he was gone, Muriel blew her nose again
and checked her face in the mirror (a disaster). She
felt a tingling in her skin, a kind of exultant but
very ordinary arrival: the molecules of the world
aligning themselves as they did after crying. On the
kitchen counter, at home, a chicken was thawing
on a plate, but here she was on Heatley Street. She
could feel his kiss at the corner of her eye. He must
have tasted her tears.

What are you doing? Muriel said to herself, and as
though to punctuate the thought, a flock of crows
crossed the upper windshield, like black leaves.

Somewhere between returning the mirror to
its proper angle and returning the Kleenex pack
to the glove compartment, she caught sight of the
boy's bag on the floor. He had not taken it with
him. She leaned over and looked up at the house.
Flimsy gate, some pampas grass beside the stone
lion. The boy was nowhere in sight. She tugged
the bag onto her lap—it was the size and weight
of a cat—slipped the antler bone from its loop, and
opened the mouth wide. Yes, this was where the

seminal reek was coming from—hops, oolichan, a sex smell. She searched the satchel with quick, practised fingers: pamphlets, wallet, ancient Hacky Sack, implement for crushing bud, glass pipe, package of saltines, Blistex—ah! Her fingernails brushed something small and glass, wedged in the corner among cracker crumbs. A *ping* of recognition.

But then the boy was there again.

He was opening the hatchback door, thrusting in a box piled high with a sleeping bag, knitting needles, an espresso maker. He flipped a duffle bag from his back, dumped it beside the box.

"Muriel, Muriel." He got in on the passenger side and glanced down. His satchel was back on the floor at his feet. "Thank you for stopping."

"You're welcome."

"But would you mind if we made one final stop? I have to drop this stuff at my friend Drew's. It's on the way." His blue-green-flecked eyes blinked once.

"Not at all," she said.

"After that we'll see the crows."

Muriel felt white sheets of anger and humiliation pouring from her forehead, over her eyebrows, down the front of her body. She turned the key. "It would be a lot of work hauling that stuff on the bus." She saw what his game was. Crows, my ass: she was helping him move house. He must have picked her out the moment he saw her—someone motherly and useful, the sort of woman who buys expensive kale.

"So where do we go now?"

"I'll show you."

"Right."

THE last of the afternoon light had given way to the wild, ruddy blush of setting sun. They drove quickly east, taking Prior to Clark, Clark to Hastings. Grain elevators heaved into view. They passed the House of Steaks, then the Black Rook Bakery. (*Look.* He pointed to the sign. *I told you we'd see crows.*)

Night was coming out of the ground. They passed under blue-limbed trees, then the steel and boards of the roller coaster in the grounds of the PNE. The boy reached for the radio button. Bob Marley filled the car, but Muriel used the steering wheel button to turn it down.

"You don't have to drive so fast. We can still get there in time." He reached behind and snapped on his seat belt. Then he took a piece of paper from his pocket and peered at it. It was the back of the crow leaflet.

"I thought you knew how to get there."

"Everything's different in a car."

They drove under the Trans-Canada Highway,

into what looked like the used car capital of the world. Everywhere, suddenly, there were rusted Wonder Bread trucks parked beside the road.

"Are we close, Simon?"

"We're close."

"Are you sure?"

Pause.

"Simon—do you have *any* idea where we're going?"

He laughed. "All right. I was so bagged I slept through the ride. But I know what I'm doing. Trust me."

She could see the glossy strangeness of a SkyTrain terminal through the scrim of leafless trees. He gestured to the right, and she pulled onto a sloping road, bumping over potholes, passing through an area of spartan bungalows, some with windows lit, some dark.

"Turn here," he said abruptly, and they did, pulling up to park in front of a small stucco house. A basement light was on.

"I'll be right back." He unloaded his box and bag quickly, taking them around the side, and Muriel was left alone.

Directly ahead of her, in the intersection's roundabout, was a community garden filled with the ragged stems of daisies. Winter interest—that was what you called those skinny, lonely looking flowers. Through the window crack she smelled pigs and old leaves.

• • •

LATER Muriel will think about why she did what she did next. She will be in recovery mode, her entire body laced with contrition, and she will think, *How could I have? And why?* But it will never be all that easy to understand.

LATER—six months later—she and Pan will decide not to take Arabella to Europe but to take her to Morocco, a place Muriel has always wanted to visit. And after Morocco, the March break after that, they will go to Mexico, the Baja Peninsula, where they will help build houses for impoverished tomato pickers, putting Pan's contracting skills to good use. In Mexico, under a hot, pink sun, she will touch Pan again, like a blind person feeling her way across an alien, familiar landscape. The days will open up again, letting more and more light in, whether she wants them to or not.

She will go about her ordinary day—buying groceries, baking cookies—but all at once she will remember being parked half a mile farther along the rutted road, beside a Wonder Bread truck with cracked windows, the light of the Costco sign filling the windshield with ghostly light. She will remember how Simon undid the pearly snaps of her blouse, and pulled down her jeans, and how they both looked down at her little bush with its needy edges, its dark frill. She will remember how her gums felt, perfect and bony, and all her teeth, and how, after they were done, he said *hush* and *look*—and they both looked out at the sign for BC Fasteners, and the barbed-wire fence strangely spangled by small black bodies, gabbling and sighing. Already she was saying *sorry*, whispering *sorry*, and these sounds were not so different from the birds.

BUT for now she is in the car, parked in front of the stucco house. She bends quickly to the satchel and feels inside, her hand knowing the shape of the thing, pulling it out. A glass vial the size of a thimble, powder inside. She stares down at it. Her nostril hairs stand up and bitter saliva builds in her mouth. She unscrews the lid, and there it is—the acrid smell that has terrorized her life. A smell like lightning. And Alexander is hovering above her, darkly perfect, watching as she takes out her purse and rolls a twenty. Interested—yes, he is interested, and even slightly afraid, to see her coming after him in this way.

LITTLE BIRD

Though my father has been dead for seven years, sometimes I imagine him clear as life, entering the dressing room at the Ex'n'Pop bar, on Mansteinstrasse, in Schöneberg. The space isn't large, but Father manages to squeeze onto the vinyl chair between the vanity and the broken pinball machine (which Ulf, the manager, in all his wisdom, has chosen to store in the dressing room forever).

"Rudy." Father's vegetarian eyes are full of remorse. "Mutti and I have spoken." He looks at my headdress on the glass-topped table, and the tubes of rouge and greasepaint. "Your mother is worried about you, son." He smells of buckskin and bananas, the inside of his old rucksack. "*Voglein*," he whispers. *Little bird*. "We want you to come home."

Yet, when he says *home*, the word meant to convey the most meaning, he glances down, not wanting to meet my eyes. Even as a ghost he is a liar: a rift of falsity, deep as his nature, has lingered into death.

THERE was no "home," and he knows it. There were only provisional rental houses—the pink house in Brazil, the white one in Cane Vale, Barbados, where Mutti threw scalding water on a foot-long centipede she found crawling across the wall of the carport. At night the stars splashed the sky with incomprehensible patterns.

I remember Father once turning to Mutti (this was late at night, on the back veranda overlooking the cane field). "Lotte," he said, "I couldn't find my way home following these stars." Mutti, as ever, looked cool and monotone in a silk blouse and drawstring trousers. She was a slender woman with hips like a boy's, monkey-ish hands with wrinkled palms, and perfect nails. Her dark hair was pulled into a chignon so tight it tugged at the tips of her eyebrows. Father pointed out the Southern Cross, then put his head in his hands, exhausted by the gin and tonics, the evening playing Troccas, a game he did not care for, and now this last insult, this blanket of unintelligible stars.

As a *Wandervogel*, you see, a scout in the German youth movement, Father had found his way to Lapland and back. With his friends Klaus (the cloddish one) and Jutta (who had sewn the flag they carried), and others whose names I now forget, he had camped out using spruce boughs for a bed, explored the woods cradling the river Elbe, and travelled all the way to Finland, hitching rides with strangers, walking for miles, riding freight trains. At night he had been reassured by the familiar pattern of constellations set in place to guide young German wanderers: Orion, with his waist girdled in diamonds, Ursa Major, Castor and Pollux.

WE were on the run through most of my childhood—fleeing Germany for Argentina, shedding Argentina for Paraguay, escaping to Bolivia, Ecuador, Colombia, working our way in hasty, unnerving flights up the body of South America. I tried to explain this to my boyfriend, Peter, one day, describing the garden in Brazil and the weeping fig tree, *Ficus benjamina*, with roots that rose above the ground like the legs of a giant insect. He kissed my temple where the veins show. (I am blond, with delicate shoulder blades, slender arms, a tracery of veins visible beneath my skin.) "So you do have some good memories," he said. Peter distrusts the outré and sensational; his nature is to calm things down. "Yes, dear," I said, "ever so many." Peter plays tennis semi-professionally: he understands practically nothing.

But he does like a story. And so he cozied up, just as I used to with Mutti when she described the white ladies of the forest, and the princes and queens of her native Saxony. I told Peter about our pink house in Rio, the wall clothed in bougainvillea, the water dripping from the lion's head. At siesta time, with the shutters closed, I could hear the servants' laughter drift across the courtyard.

But soon the story took its inevitable sorry turn: Mutti was weeping, Father ordering the maid to pack our things. There were scenes. Mutti was exhausted, and what kind of life was this for a child. Mutti stormed off to consult the Troccas deck, but to no avail.

You are probably dying to ask: What did your father *do?* What set your family spinning into the Southern Hemisphere? What was this albatross slung around your necks? I sometimes think that there was not a time when I didn't know, but that is not the case. When I was five I didn't know. Those were the days of childhood immortality, when the very idea of death was unknown, and time was vast and uncharted, not measured into hours and half-hours. Father told me that the Easter Bunny followed us from Buenos Aires, searching me out with his basket of cream-filled eggs. He held me on his shoes and danced me around the kitchen table. He got down next to me, brown eyes beaming with kindness, and sang me a song about cheese mites. Looking into my face, seeing my belief in him, what a relief I must have been!

He was brimful of vitality, a great believer in the importance of roughage. (He even mixed sawdust with his camp food during the war, a teaspoon at a time, to stay regular.) He had lost his hair from the tight helmet he had to wear every day (yet another terrifying consequence of war), but this meant I had a good view of his ears, which he could wriggle by moving a muscle in each temple. Most importantly, he showed me his trick of springing onto his hands, then walking about as though his palms were the soles of his feet. He spent hours holding my feet against his chest, teaching me to root my palms into the ground, find my centre of balance. "You'll kill the child," Mutti said. "He'll break his neck." But as you can see, that didn't happen. Father and I were wonders to ourselves with this art, displayed on the beach or on a park lawn, of leaping onto our hands and walking side by side, upside down.

Yet the other thing was there too. It expressed itself as an absence beneath my ribs, a need to go to the bathroom—what I felt the time I got sunstroke: the stink of diarrhea in my bedroom, fig pods clacking against the shutters, and my parents' voices, disembodied. They might have been in my head, they were that close, Father's whispers beating back Mutti's, whose voice, lower pitched, was like waves on the beach, not the crashing ones at dusk, but the medium ones on a sandy shore.

"We're all tired, Heinrich."

More lapping.

Then Mutti: "I wish to God we had stayed."

I could imagine her standing over Father, his head in his palms, vanquished. For a while, even as a grown-up, this image made me terribly sad, until I realized that if Father had been painted naked in this pose by a kitsch Romantic painter, he would have been the picture of biblical sorrow—*Job sobs in grief over his trials.* That's what I mean about Father's streak of dishonesty: it inhabited even the poses he struck to represent guilt.

IN Barbados we lived in a new suburb called Cane Vale, just three houses built so far, on a plateau overlooking a cane field. It was about a mile from Oistins Beach. While the rains lashed down, the plateau was covered in a copperlike sheen, and the village boys didn't bring their animals to graze.

Then the rainy season ended, and I walked out the door, past the steaming flower beds and onto the school bus, where, to my amazement, one Sanford Fortescu, with downy blossom of cheek and pouting lips of a Botticelli angel, invited me to his house after school.

Sanford was the prince of Christ Church Parish Boys Academy—an absolute dark prince of power and prestige, though by and large he didn't abuse his authority, never throwing the younger boys' hymn books in puddles as Miguel Santos did. Like Prince Hal, he was universally loved, and though one day (so we felt) he would wear the crown of king, still he deigned to go among the rabble. He was the champion rounders player, best at cricket, captain of the rugby team. When he ran his legs spun like a comic strip figure's—forming wheels of air. He was, in his excellence, the sort of boy Mutti would have liked for a son, and Father would have embraced for the *Wandervogels*, except for the fact, rather crucial, that Sanford was Jewish.

For the most part Mutti's anti-Semitism was casual, almost respectful: she appreciated survival. But in Barbados it was different. At least a third of the boys at my school were Jewish, from families that had immigrated to the Caribbean at the end of the nineteenth century, making it rich in wholesale exports. Some, like Sanford's family, lived on Oistins Row, in houses overlooking the beach. They had to cross the road to swim, and the beach was rocky, and you couldn't put a foot down but you'd step on a prickly sea urchin (in which case you'd have to urinate on the puncture wound), but still: east of Oistins meant prestige. This acted on Mutti, bringing out old humiliations, how her parents had lost their property to a Jewish mortgage company. It seemed hard for her that she, an aristocrat, did not live on Oistins Row.

Now here was Sanford Fortescu, leaning forward in his bus seat, asking if I understood the homework. We had to compose stories from magazine pictures stuck to pieces of cardboard. I took one glance at Sanford's scene (a cat by a hearth, pie steaming on a window ledge) and a story started to grow: I peopled his cottage with a couple of gnomes, invented a prince and a dragon, filled the lane with a pageant of hunters, pages, trumpeters, children strewing petals.

"How did you come up with that?" Sanford said. "When I look at this picture I see a cat." He lowered his voice. "You're Rudy, aren't you. Do you suppose you want to meet me at Oistins—bike to my house after school? Course you'd have to put up with my five sisters."

Five. Had I heard right? It sounded like a fairy tale.

"Oh, I have five, all right." He listed them off on his fingers: "Tamara, Rosalia, Lucia, Luisa, Seraphina. They're all older than me, except Seraphina. She's a pipsqueak. Stands about this height—" He raised a hand to his shoulder. "She's horribly spoiled."

Seraphina. Isn't that lovely? I asked where her name came from, but Sanford just said: "My parents, of course. Didn't yours name you? Her hair is your colour," he added. "She can sit on her pigtails."

The names of the older sisters sounded dank and mature, but Seraphina's glowed. To this day I see Hebrew letters in a margin, arcane notes regarding spheres of heaven, seraphim and cherubim.

Getting off the bus, Sanford repeated his invitation. Then off he strode, trailing clouds of glory.

COME home with me. One might discern a pattern: Father saying those words bold as life from the shadow of that hulking pinball machine in the dressing room, and Sanford whispering them years ago on the school bus. If I were the type, I'd see an analyst, pour out the contents of my life, hawks and hand grenades, Mutti's torchlit parades mixing with Father's groans. Then there is Peter—poor thing. Why is it that in every relationship a dismal moment arrives when one's lover suggests the seaside? The Baltic, with its dreary pebbles, becomes an absolute must-see. I think Peter imagines the sea spray washing us clean, scrubbing the crenellations of our furrowed brains.

Peter is six foot two, wiry and athletic. He wears button-down shirts and high-waisted corduroys that do not do justice to his lovely ass. He is a technician in a computer firm, not a shoe salesman or a cobbler, though his last name is Shumaker, which I find charming: as though Peter left me late at night to make shoes in a little shop, accompanied by elves. His parents were Presbyterians from Munich. According to Peter they were persecuted for their beliefs during the war. I had no idea that Presbyterians were a persecuted minority. Can you picture it? Clandestine Presbyterian meetings in the dead of night. The handing out of inflammatory Presbyterian literature. But Peter believes adamantly in these tales of Presbyterian derring-do, so I do not pop his balloon.

It isn't just me at the seaside that Peter wants: it is me stripped of my finery. As though there were a greater truth to seeing me in jeans and a badly fitting T-shirt. Yet Peter knows what I'm capable of creating—or should I say, of teasing into the open. Each Friday at the Ex'n'Pop I push my way from the dressing room, through the crowd on bar stools and at tables (the place, let me tell you, is a lot more crowded than it ever gets on Punk Night). The stage is at the front of the bar, next to the door. It is an old window alcove, backed with corrugated tin shutters, but we have draped it with plum-coloured velvet curtains. Up I go, balancing the feathered head-dress ever so carefully. Then I dance, shedding fish-net stockings, taking forever to unzip my organza dress. When I'm down to my G-string, I spring onto my hands (that old trick, no easy feat in that tiny space), and yes, the headdress stays in place, it's practically nailed to my head. And all this is fine, it impresses the Beck-drinking crowd. But this is not what they've come for, what has made me, I confess, a sensation. It is when I stop, and the piped-in music dies, and I ask Ulf to pass me a bar stool—this is when I make them ache. Even Peter that first time, wandering into the Ex'n'Pop with tennis friends, the straightest gay man in Berlin, his lean mouth, which I know to be kind, pursed in contempt, even he ached when I sang my "Little Bird" song.

I got the idea from a photo in a *National Geographic*, which I found at my dentist's office on the Ku'damm: it showed a bird with turquoise, cobalt and brown-speckled plumage hanging upside down from the limb of a tree. *Prince Rudolph's Blue Bird of*

Paradise. All the way home I was so excited, I kept swallowing the paste the dentist had scrubbed onto my teeth. I saw Father and me upside down walking across the sand. I saw the Hanged Man in Mutti's Troccas deck, dangling from a gallows tree. (*No, he isn't dead,* Mutti whispered to me. *Look, the gallows is sprouting branches.*) I heard Father's tenor rising out of nowhere, singing the folk song he had learned in the *Wandervogels.* Sometimes he sang it at my bedside as a lullaby. Sometimes Mutti joined him, both of them looking down at me tenderly.

> *"Wenn ich ein Vöglein wär*
> *Und auch zwei Flüglein hätt,*
> *Flog ich zu dir."*

> *If I were a little bird*
> *And I had two little wings,*
> *I would fly to you.*

It is a touching folk song, quite famous, which many composers, including Beethoven, have set to music. The last stanza goes like this:

> *There is not one hour of the night*
> *When my heart is not awake*
> *And thinking of you.*

———

SANFORD and I biked past the Oistins bar with its picnic tables out front. The locals shouted at us, acknowledging my flare of blond hair, which attracted attention wherever I went. A playing card clacked in Sanford's spokes. Between the bar and the motel I glimpsed the sea. Herculean, I thought, liking the word and all that it implied of muscles, and Greece, and uncomplicated strength.

In memory this scene is all blue sky and blue sea, but next moment the sky has darkened. Frantically we bicycle up the slope while things from our lives blow past us, like the tornado scene in *The Wizard of Oz*. Poor us! Seraphina pitches by in her blue dress, and Mutti, shuffling her deck, and Father pulling on his boots. At the base of the seaside cliff, the shoreline is coated with the brittle, cupped shells of sea urchins—the size of cat skulls.

Word had gotten out on our sunny island. Pilar Romeros, a friend of my mother's, had come to the house the afternoon before, wearing a pink-and-green pantsuit with paisley swirls. I let her in, seeing with alarm the paisley outline of her crotch. From the bar in the living room, just inside the sliding glass doors, I watched as she and Mutti took turns shuffling the cards, pausing to take sips of their gin and tonics.

Pilar riffled the deck expertly. "It is grossly unfair."

"My heart is breaking," Mutti whispered.

"Who is this 'eyewitness'?"

"Rudy has been happy."

"Enough."

Pilar turned the cards over: swords and pentacles. More swords. I strained to see the layout. Pilar flipped the last card: yes, there he was, the Hanged Man, dangling upside down from the gallows tree. Mutti laughed out loud, it was so awful.

"Are you satisfied?" she said. "My mother used to call this card the Traitor."

I lay down on the tile floor with its beige-and-white cloudy swirls. A glass of Coke had spilled there once and a mass of ants had swarmed in, covering the spillage with legs and bodies. *Leiscec.* That was the word that had gotten out. The word I wasn't supposed to hear. *Leiscec*—a Lithuanian village. I always imagine it tinted: a green sun shining on green fields, green houses.

So, even on that bike ride to Sanford's house, with the sea over our right shoulders and the sky above, there was an enormous eye floating above us like a second sun, fleshily glistening. The eye of the eyewitness.

We cycled up the driveway, past palms with trunks as thick as elephants' legs, then threw our bikes on the gravel by the side of the house. We descended three stone steps to enter a cool kitchen with a stone floor. Standing behind a table was a heavy-breasted black woman wearing a flowered skirt. She held a knife.

"He's all right." Sanford slid into a chair at the table. "He's my new friend."

"Where's your old friend?"

"Miguel? I hate Miguel."

"That boy's no end of trouble." She hacked a papaya in two.

"She's imagining that's Miguel's head."

Flash. Chop. Flash. The papaya was cut in eighths.

"I hate papaya." I could hear a younger child in Sanford's voice.

"You supposed to eat fruit."

"But not papaya."

"It ain't ackee season." The cook took two slices of white bread from the breadbox and sprinkled them with chocolate, then put the plates in front of us.

Sanford had flaws; I could see this now. He had been spoiled by his many sisters. He was rude to the chocolate-sprinkling cook. Yet seeing these defects, I liked him more: they added interest, as moles do on perfect faces. As we ate, I wondered what part of this scene got its character from being Jewish. Was it Jewish to sprinkle chocolate on bread? Was it Jewish to have a servant like this, a gatekeeper to the house above? Was the stone floor Jewish? I kept wondering what the sisters' bedrooms were like, and the study, where I pictured Sanford's father bent over a Talmudic script. I felt equal portions of fear and desire at the thought of the fiercely spoiled Seraphina, with braids she could tuck under her bum. I listened for footsteps in the hall, but as soon as we were done eating, Sanford gestured for me to follow him out again, across the back lawn to a trail. It led to a garden house made of whitewashed wood. I followed him in.

Light filtered through the banana leaves outside. A lizard scurried across the wall. Piles of mildewed boxes filled each corner of the room.

"See?" Sanford reached into one and pulled out a large-format comic book. "They're my sisters'. My aunt in England sends them."

I bent and picked out a comic book. *The Adventures of Julia James: School Girl Sleuth.* The cover showed a girl in a skirt and blazer jumping a stile.

"They're good." Sanford took a stack and placed them on the floor. He lay down, his head on the pile of comics, then asked me to toss him a bunch. I pulled out a dozen comics, brought them over, and he smoothed them into a neat pile, placing them on his stomach. "You'll like them, Rudy."

I took a pile for my head, another for my stomach, and lay on the floor beside him. I heard the shifting of branches, a skitter on the roof.

"Monkeys," Sanford said.

Their toenails scratched the roof. The stack of comics on Sanford's stomach rose and fell. I opened a comic book. Julia James, head prefect, listened as schoolgirls gathered round her, accusing a second-form child of stealing a necklace. It turned out (thanks to Julia's sharp eyes) that a crow had stolen the sparkly necklace from the top of a wardrobe and carried it to its nest. Then Julia uncovered the identity of a mystery hurdler (Who is that girl leaping stiles in the distance? We need her for the track team!). It was the baker's daughter, delivering loaves at dawn. Each story ended with Julia and the other prefects sprawled in the common room eating crumpets.

I read until I was glutted with a sickly sweet disgust. Sanford seemed glutted too. He nudged my arm. "Stop. It's boring now."

He rolled over and put his wrist beside mine. "You're so pale."

"I know."

He turned my wrist over, tracing his fingertip on a vein. I watched him do this, willing him to keep going, but his finger stopped. "Let's arm wrestle," he said.

We rolled onto our stomachs and clasped hands. The struggle lasted a moment, then he had my arm down. His hand kept clasping mine, which hurt.

"Give?"

"Give."

"Good. Do you want to leg wrestle?"

We lay on our backs, my head beside his feet, our hips touching, then we each raised a leg, linking our ankles. The hairs of his thighs brushed my skin.

"One, two, three—" He pulled my leg over. I sprawled across him, my ankle pinned beneath his.

"You're not very strong, are you. Seraphina puts up more of a fight."

We lay side by side, panting; then he jumped up and straddled me, not sitting on my stomach, hovering just above. He pinned my arms and looked down, his breath in my face.

"So now I get to ask you questions. Okay?"

"Okay."

"You're not going to like it, Rudy."

"Okay."

"Rudy?" He gave my arms a pinch.

"What?"

"You're not going to like it."

That seemed almost impossible. But I nodded to show I understood.

I thought he might lean down and kiss me, he

put his face so close. Instead he whispered, "Miguel says your father's a Nazi."

Cold liquid washed down my spine. Nothing had changed, except that his face held a deeper concentration. He waited for me to speak.

"Is it true?"

I wriggled and he put more weight on my arms. "You're supposed to submit to questioning."

"I am."

"Then don't keep moving. Now listen: the fellows at school want to know. They say it's true. There's a village with a weird name where all sorts of people got killed."

Again a chill rushed to my tailbone, an ache.

"They say he got the children to line up in front of a pit."

I rolled from side to side, getting my arm free, but he pinned it again. "That's a lie, Sanford. Miguel's a filthy bastard."

"Is it a lie? Tell me."

"Anything he did, it was following orders. Like anyone would do in a war."

"Have you asked him? Have you said to your old man: 'Look, did you shoot a whole pile of children? Did you stab them with bayonets?'"

"Stop it!"

"It's not me that did it. It's your old man."

"No he didn't!" I couldn't believe this was happening; it was nightmarish, but also real, something I'd waited for. His penis felt hard as he straddled me. He leaned forward, rope-burning my forearms.

"Does he have medals? An Iron Cross?"

"If I tell you, will you let me up?"

"I might."

He looked down with the demanding face of an angel, beautiful, pouty and fierce.

"He has an Iron Cross. He got it for being brave."

Sanford inched his crotch closer to my face, pressing down on my arms. "But how do you know?"

"Stop it!"

"Does he explain? Does he say why? Miguel says your dad threw children up in the air and they landed on bayonets—don't you want to know why?"

As he lightened his grip, I got my hand free and knocked him off balance. Bucking and pushing, I managed to scramble to my feet, where I stood like a boxer, fists up, expecting him to lunge. But he just laughed.

"You're daft," he said. "A daft midget. Go home."

And me thinking I'd been invited to eat chocolate sprinkles and read *The Adventures of Julia James*!

I NEVER did meet Seraphina, or any of the sisters, though for years Sanford's family turned up in dreams. Once I rode my bike up Sanford's driveway

and it thinned to a path at the back of the property, overhung by trees. *Trembling aspen,* a voice said,
and I knew I was near Leiscec. When I reached the
garden house, moss had grown on the eaves. It was
twilight, and through the windowpane a light shone
invitingly. I put an eye to the glass and saw Sanford
and his father and five sisters.

Seraphina was turning to and fro, holding the
hem of her filmy dress, admiring herself in a mirror.
Her gold hair hung down her back, and her skin was
lit from within. She must have just said something to
the others, because both Sanford and his father were
smiling at her indulgently. Then Seraphina began to
twirl, making the skirt of her dress fan out, tilting
her chin up and laughing.

I stared in, my task simply to watch, to bear witness to her beautiful spinning.

THAT night, when I got home from Sanford's I left
my bike in the carport, where Mutti had scalded the
foot-long centipede. I passed through the wrought-
iron gate, which Father locked at night to keep out
robbers and cutthroats. In the living room Mutti and
Father were silent as the dead; Father was curled on
the vinyl couch, his back to the room, and Mutti sat
at the card table. I knew by how she held her head
that she was angry with me.

Father turned over, shielding his eyes from the overhead lamp. He gave me a smile, weak but hopeful. "You're home late."

"I went to a friend's." I put my school bag by the bar.

"Which friend?" Mutti didn't look up from her spread.

"He lives on Oistins Row."

Mutti flicked a card onto the table. I knew the word in her head, *Juden*, though she didn't speak it. What did it matter now? Oistins Row was already in the past. In another three weeks we would be gone, boxes packed, visas arranged. There were friends of friends with an apartment in Belize.

We would continue our wanderings—Belize, Antigua, Puerto Vallarta—until one bright morning Mutti and Father would swerve to avoid a box of chickens that fell from a multicoloured bus, running headlong into the archway of a concrete overpass. This was when I was seventeen, in the second district of Guatemala City. It feels like a long time ago.

But for now Sanford's voice rang in my ears, the demands of a wild and petulant angel. *Don't you ever ask why? Doesn't he explain?* I went to the bathroom and looked in the mirror.

I could hear their voices rising—Mutti's hissing,

Father's cajoling. I opened Mutti's polka-dotted box of talcum. The puff inside was heavy with powder.

The rest was natural. Just play. A pleasure which, when it arrives, feels so natural you wonder why you waited, or what you could have been afraid of. I smeared shadow on my lids with the tip of my index finger. I applied lipstick. Then I darkened my eyebrows like Sanford's. Even that first time I could feel how much the pleasure had to do with mixing and matching, using what was there. Hung over the bathtub rail, among Mutti's nylons, was a silk scarf she used to wrap the Troccas deck. Could I not use that to wrap my loins? The word *loins*, its biblical sound, reminding me of Sanford wrenching my leg over with his, one thrust of his hips. I said it again:

And he covered his loins.
And he girded his loins.

They were calling me now, Mutti and Father, wanting to announce the decision to leave Barbados, or perhaps Mutti had decided to forbid me from visiting Oistins Row after all. I will never know. I took a breath and emerged from the bathroom wearing nothing but that scarf and a pair of Mutti's feathered slippers. I swayed down the hall, clippety-clip, my heart beating like mad, and wafted into the room like the swan prince himself. I stood before them.

Mutti laid down her cards, mouth falling open. Oh, the sorrow on her lined face, lips creased where the lipstick ran upward, tiny capillaries full of blood. She leapt up, instinct making her want to shield me. Father stood by the sliding glass doors, a newspaper in his hand, his view partly blocked by the bar counter. I could have turned, scurried back up the hall, covered by Mutti's fluttering. Instead, I swayed past her and faced my father, my chin raised to receive the benediction, as it were, of his taking me in.

Deep disappointment, that was what I saw: the deepest disappointment of a loving father in an unworthy son. That came as a blow, and almost knocked me back up the hall to the bathroom. Then his eyes grew colder. He looked me up and down, a crooked smile on his face: a smile of shock, I see now.

"Heinrich, please. Do something!" This was Mutti.

The molecules of his face swam. "Rudy." He shook his head. "I don't know what you are doing—go and wash!"

"No, Father."

"You're frightening your mother. Go now."

"No."

The anger welling up through his body must have felt good, righteous even, as it filled him to the brim with conviction. To see such a wrong, a twist in the fabric of nature, must have been shocking indeed; but how good, how electrifying, to realize you could do something about it.

"Change! This second!"

"No, Father."

"Do something!" Mutti cried, and at her hissed command I saw my father pass out of confusion, over the bridge, to the country of perfect clarity. He came toward me, reaching for his belt.

SO I know the power of a good outfit, believe me.

And perhaps now you understand why I won't go to the seaside, to trudge beside Peter, who wears an ugly hat. I have my work cut out for me at the Ex'n'Pop, under the disco balls, against my backdrop of velvet and corrugated tin.

I step onto the stage on Friday nights, the feathers of my headdress flaming in the spotlight. *Careful or you will burn.* I take in the feel of the beer-drinking crowd, then I narrow my eyes, willing suspension of disbelief, and look, it works, because now (intake of breath) we are transported to a desert beneath the canopy of a southern sky. I strip and play and flaunt my limbs, but one must imagine it all with more fanfare and more terror, with chords of Beethoven thrumming in one's ears. A camel kneels on its knobby forelegs, and I straddle it easily, rubbing my loins against its hump. Up it bears me like a prince, and the sky sings with its diamond glitter, and the black slaves and white slaves, concubines and eunuchs, stand back in awe, waiting.

Child king, they whisper. *Little bird. Voglein.*

A SMALL HAUNTING

The haunting started on a Monday. Anna remembered that later—how the morning had begun with all of Monday's chores and rush: getting Michael and Juliette out of bed, making salami sandwiches, pouring orange juice into portable juice boxes. Juliette's cheek was criss-crossed with pillow marks as she came into the kitchen clutching her stuffed elephant. Her ridiculously plush lips and bow mouth—*I can't find my underwear!*

Anna moved through her tasks like a life-giving machine: sandwiches; underwear; Thermos of Scotch broth for Kevin (husband), who had joined Weight Watchers with her but didn't attend the meetings; Cheerios poured into a bowl; milk spilled and wiped; juice spilled and wiped. Michael, coming to breakfast with his Game Boy, tweaked her heart with concern. Then she kissed Kevin at the door.

His lips, plush and large like Juliette's, were lightly freckled.

It was when she returned to the kitchen and was clearing cereal bowls that Anna saw the photograph in *The Vancouver Sun*. Looking across the table, she didn't understand it at first. She came around and picked up the paper. There were dead cows in the picture, twenty or perhaps thirty, and they had been shovelled into a pile and set aflame. *In Ireland*, the caption said. *Mad cow disease.* Anna stood for a moment, absorbing the image, the exposed udders, cloven hooves helplessly poking the air, then she called out to Juliette to brush her teeth.

Anna walked the children to school, dropping Michael at the playground, taking her place with the other mothers at the chain-link fence. Misty rain collected on their raincoats. Like Anna, these women were in their late thirties, heavy in the hips, swollen, she thought, from years of mothering. Some had frizzy hair, others had pulled theirs back in utilitarian ponytails. Anna herself was blond, with calm features, and a florid beauty that struck her at times as a bit heavy-handed. She was a children's book illustrator and her drawings were thoughtful and painstaking, woodblocks, pen and ink, but she herself was blowsy, as though the artist had gone a little wild. Her cheeks, subject to eczema, were often ruddy. Sometimes, glimpsing herself in the security monitor at the bank or in the mirror of the fish store window, she was reminded of a bosomy peasant woman from *The Illustrated Brothers Grimm*.

She made sure Michael had found some friends to talk to, then she walked Juliette to her classroom. It smelled of white glue and the inside of rubber boots. Anna bent to hug her daughter goodbye and then left the school, still breathing in the girl's sweet scalp. She crossed Sixteenth Avenue, stepping over chestnuts that had fallen to the boulevard. Nothing was wrong yet. At Tenth Avenue she cut through the gardens of Our Lady of Perpetual Help and approached the house.

Later she considered the sequence. Stepping onto the dewy grass, feeling it soak the leather of her clogs. Shivering. Looking down at the house, which, from this perspective, always gave her pleasure. The church lawn was sloped, not enough for sledding in winter but enough to make the children break into a run. The house was across the road: a Cape Cod Colonial shaped like a barn, white with green shutters and a red door, and graced by huge maples full of starlings and squirrels, a life that went on almost completely unobserved in the topmost canopy.

Anna felt it—a pricking of skin along her spine, hairs rising at the back of her neck—before she saw anything. She glanced at the second-floor bathroom window. A child's face watched her through the glass. Anna stopped, blinked—was that what she had done? She couldn't remember later—and the child's face was gone.

At first Anna thought it was Juliette, though this information, that it was Juliette, made no sense; and besides, this child did not *seem* like Juliette. Still, Anna dashed across the grass, over the embankment, across the road. She fumbled out her key, inserted it in the lock, sensing as she did this, heart pounding in her ears, the thing on the other side of the door, laughing soundlessly, clutching its sides.

"Juliette?"

Anna twisted the key and pushed open the door. A bar of sunlight streamed through the transom window, breaking into pieces on the treads of the stairs. Not a sound but the fridge ticking, the way it did every morning of their lives.

NOTHING. It had been nothing. There had been no face at the bathroom window (though it had struck her deep, that look: a blow to the chest). There had been no laughing child on the other side of the door.

And yet the haunting continued.

On Tuesday someone took a bite from every furry kiwi in the bowl on the counter. Who did this?

Anna demanded. They all denied it. Maybe it was mice, Kevin suggested, but each bite was the size of a quarter, and not one kiwi was eaten whole; each was just tasted and left, as though to say, *Fuck you and your perfect fruit.*

On Wednesday the rain poured down in bucketfuls. The furnace began to bang like a kettledrum, the fridge continued to tick—the house, in its cacophony, resembling a brass band.

Returning home from the school drop-off, Anna made a pot of tea and took the stairs to the attic. A neatly tacked seagrass runner led to her clean space: the metal drafting table topped in glass, the glossy white floorboards, the collection of Mexican tumblers in which she was forcing narcissus. She had seen a picture in a magazine of a room with floors like this, above a canal in Amsterdam, and she had tried to replicate the sense of calm. She was of Dutch ancestry; the picture had spoken to her.

Both her parents had left Holland after the war, moving to West Vancouver, where they became part of the expatriate Dutch community. They filled their basement larder with Gouda rounds and smoky coils of peppered salami. Anna remembered being sent downstairs to fetch a cheese round from a wooden box packed with straw, the smell of the room, salty and tantalizing. Her parents, she thought now, staring down at her cross-hatchings in ink, had stocked that pantry to ward off famine.

She had been commissioned to make a series of illustrations for a book of *ABC*s. She was on *C*. She had drawn a Siamese cat gingerly dipping its paw in a saucer of milk. The cat was a black shadow, but you could tell it was Siamese from the length of its body, its long neck and pointed ears. In testing the saucer the cat had pulled it forward, spilling milk (the paper showing through) on the black floor.

The picture was not coming. *A* had been fine (an alligator in sunglasses and a straw sunhat), and *B* simple but effective (bananas on a wood-grained windowsill). But *C* was giving Anna a clog in her throat. Stepping back from the table she saw that the cat's haunches were too large for its body. The cat had a fat ass.

She didn't want to work on the alphabet, anyway. Her mind was full of memories of her mother, now dead, and her mother's friends, with their opinionated, accented voices, their almost rude way of speaking. Why think of them now? Because they were in her head, that was all, suddenly present. Her mother's voice: *Anna, bring the cheese—why do you take so long?*

She remembered being at Bachelor Bay with them all, a pebbled beach in Howe Sound. She was about twelve, with fine hair to her waist. When she moved, the insides of her legs did not rub together. She dove in and swam to a log boom, where she lay on her back feeling the wash of the boom as the ferry waves hit, the shagginess of the bark against her skin. Afterward, as she swam back toward the mothers on the beach, the tips of her white, puckered fingers feathered the green water. All but her head was invisible, and she could see the mothers clearly, laughing and talking, flapping sand from towels. They were dressed in silly outfits like clowns, one-piece bathing suits in red and white stripes, lime green and neon orange. Her own mother wore a bathing cap covered in flashing sequins.

These women with their sulky, recalcitrant bodies, with pubic bushes escaping their coverings, with breasts that sagged, these women, these *mothers*—they didn't have a shred of nobility. That was what Anna had thought, swimming toward them, and even now she remembered the electric anger she'd felt, watching them parading farcically on the beach. They looked, one and all, as though they had lost themselves, beaten by their children's demands, by the new algebra, by men, by the very ease of their lives.

Fat women. That's what they were.

Yet once, at a different picnic, she had heard her mother's friend Eveline say, in response to the bounty laid out on a blanket (potato salad, chicken salad, eggs and cheese and pickles), *To think we ate nettle soup!* Nettle soup! They all remembered it. It had turned their mouths green, tasted bitter. *One step up from stone soup,* Eveline said. More laughter. They dished food onto Tupperware plates and told the children to get out of the water, to stay out for an hour after eating.

Anna shoved her pen into the inkpot. She could join those mothers on the beach now: she was their size and heft. Under her loose T-shirt she felt the Caesarean scar, a six-inch swath of her stomach frozen from the suturing after Michael's birth, nerve endings that would never re-knit. Why think about it all? It was the cat's fat ass that had done it. She took up the vellum sheet and ripped it in two.

Maybe she should think of another, better word that began with *C. Catatonic? Cacophony?* That would be something: an alphabet book to terrify children. *A* might be for *Apoplexy. B* for *Barn-burning.* She could imagine the woodcut figure of the fire-starter stealing into the barn, a lit match in his hand. Behind her, a shuffle of feet. Suppressed laughter. Anna hurried across the floor and looked down the stairs. Then she slammed the studio door.

———

SHE woke the next morning, Thursday, with the girl's voice in her ear. Even with closed eyes Anna felt her—sour breath on her face, dirty teeth, a constrained panic in her heart.

You should slit your wrists.

Anna sat up, grabbing at the sheet. Kevin opened an eye.

"You're jumpy."

"A nightmare." Anna turned to him. "I saw a child."

"Children can be frightening." His eye closed again.

She wanted to say she had seen a child the day before too, and the day before that, but she didn't know how to explain it, and besides, Kevin seemed to have fallen back asleep. She cuddled against him, then they both flipped, and he snuggled against her back, cupping her breast. His underarms smelled, not unpleasantly, of baked beans. Slowly, as though working a complex and ancient fountain, he began to press her breast. He squeezed, pressed, and then improvised with a light jiggle. Anna felt a flicker of irritation.

"Don't." She lifted his hand away.

ON the way to school Michael said, "I've made it into the seventh circle of Hell." He was referring to his video game, Diablo, a battle with the living dead.

Anna kissed his head, then watched him cross the playground. In Juliette's classroom a pixieish girl climbed onto the art table.

"Everybody, listen!" For a small child she had a booming voice. All commotion stopped—the mothers stripping their children of boots and raincoats, the teacher distributing yellow excursion forms. "I know where I came from!" the child cried out, full of potency and glee. "Guess where? Guess where? Guess where?"

"We couldn't possibly." The teacher gave Anna a half-smile. "Why don't you tell us, Maeve."

"My daddy says I came out of my mother's big fat hairy vagina!"

Walking home in the rain, Anna passed a funeral at the Catholic church, six pallbearers carrying a dove-gray casket: the coffin of a woman. When Anna reached her house, she could feel the child on the other side of the door, pressed close, waiting.

"I'm coming in." Anna's heart hammered, sounding like a giant's footsteps in her ears. On the other side, the creature held a pair of pointed nail scissors. Sallow face, green mouth, hollow below the ribs.

"Here I come." Anna took the keys from her purse, jingling them while the child waited, scissors in hand. But no, Anna couldn't do it. She stood, keys in her palm, then she turned and walked back along the concrete pathway, across the church lawn. *But where will you go,* she asked herself, *if you can't finish the breakfast cleanup, brew yourself a pot of tea, and head upstairs to make your careful bird's-feet markings on vellum?*

Anna trudged along Tenth Avenue, cars splashing her. When she reached the railway tracks at Arbutus Street she stood looking down at them, smelling the creosote, then she began to follow them south. She could see into the backyards of people's houses, a different view than from the road: stacks of wood, clotheslines, garbage cans, a henhouse.

The rails were slippery from the rain, so she stepped on the ties, finding it hard to match her stride to their spread. This reminded her of a boyfriend she'd had years before who'd lived in an abandoned milk truck on a lake near Pemberton. He used to walk the railway tracks every day, four miles to the gas station to get his food, which he sometimes paid for and sometimes stole. He had become very good at balancing on the rails, jumping from one to the other. Anna had tried to jump from rail to rail too, but wasn't nearly as good at it, and he had told her, with an ascetic's dignity, that it would come only if she practised daily.

The rain slowed, then stopped. Her hair was soaked. Her face was soaked. Her chest was soaked.

Her feet squished in her running shoes. But she couldn't go home. *What is happening to me?* she thought. It seemed to her that if her mother were alive, Anna would ask her this question, pleading for the answer; though in fact, when her mother was alive, they had, for years, moved in separate spheres. It was only in the wild dusk since her death that Anna ached for her. Now, under the overcast sky, her mother seemed to be everywhere: in the grasses, in the telephone poles, the plastic bag flapping in the barbed-wire fence beside the track. Everywhere and nowhere. Anna moved down the rails, stepping, skipping a tie, stepping, crying. She had been lulled by her mother's fullness, her hips and loose breasts (she never wore proper underclothes), the gust of long hair, braided unceremoniously, tied with a blue elastic saved from a bunch of green onions.

IT was night now, and Anna was at home again. She was sitting on the bed, telling Kevin the story from beginning to end, as he changed out of his suit. He had been at a meeting, then gone for drinks with a client. It was close to nine at night. Anna described the face at the window, the walk in the rain, the sorrow, so deep, which had blossomed out of nowhere, like a sunspot, consuming her vision.

"I miss her so much," she said, meaning her mother.

Kevin sat heavily on the bed. Anna could smell beer on his breath. Soon he'd get up, say good-night to the children, but for the moment he was calm and listening, taking their marriage seriously. He gripped her neck, giving it a massagelike squeeze. She felt tears rise. What hurt the most, she wanted to say, was that the girl was just so *mean*, her hate so precise, like slipping a needle in to touch bone.

"It's because we have so much," Anna said. "That's why she hates us."

"She? This ghost, you mean."

"Because we forget about the others—"

"What others?"

"You know." The starving children, she meant. The refugees. The nettle-eaters. She had followed the rails for miles, beyond the houses, across a trestle bridge, past the garbage dump, the backs of warehouses and pulp mills. By the river, she had looked down the embankment at a squalid timbered hut, thinking that nobody could possibly live there, then seen a teenage girl emerge from it, a Musqueam girl, in a yellow-and-green cheerleading outfit.

Kevin rubbed her back.

"Anna," he said gently.

She knew from the way he stroked, in careful circles, what was to follow: that all this might be a mood, a fractious swing into darkness that, while always unexpected, did *seem* to come monthly.

"It's not that," she said sharply. "Don't make light of it."

He looked abashed but sly, as though he knew the cause of it all but had to follow her lead. And in fact her PMS did have a way of sneaking up on her, skinning her, leaving her bleak and terrified by her own life, though—and why was this?—through some deep-seated refusal to adjust, every one of her periods seemed to arrive as a surprise.

Just then, Juliette called out, wanting to be tucked in. Kevin rose in relief. At the door he turned.

"You know, Anna," he said, "you have these highs and lows, and you always say, once you work through them, that they fuel your work. Have you been drawing?"

She felt a red spot of anger between her eyebrows. "I saw a ghost," she said. "You're not listening."

But after he left the room, she felt her anger receding like a dank tide. She did have highs and lows, it was true. And they did fuel her work. She covered her eyelids with her palms. On the walk, after seeing the Musqueam girl, Anna had tasted something metallic beneath her tongue and felt a heavy creaking in her hips, like a boat pulling against its anchor. She had found a gas station and asked for the key. Under the fluorescent lights, she had pulled down her jeans and there it was—a spot of bright blood on her underwear.

Anna pressed hard with her palms and groaned. She wanted it to be more than that, she wanted clarity, she wanted the girl back right that second, so she could see the lines and angles of her face—the green lips half-open, the sallow cheeks. But it was no use. She could hear Kevin reading *The House at Pooh Corner* to their daughter: "You're a Bear of Very Little Brain," she heard. "A Bear of Very Little Brain."

Anna got up, straightened the duvet cover and crossed the hallway to Michael's room.

"Five minutes," she said.

"I'm about to slay Lazarus." He didn't look up from the screen. A figure of doom was reflected in his glasses.

Anna went into the bathroom and stood looking out over the lace curtain, taking up the exact position where the girl had first stood. The churchyard was covered in frost. She imagined herself crossing the grass, looking up, startled.

In the very prime of her motherhood, in the thick underwater heat of it, a skinny ghost was haunting her. And Anna couldn't explain the reasons, any more than she could explain why there were times when her life felt full and times when it was a bone scraped clean of meat, her marriage appearing, in stark clarity, as a skeleton. And this cycle seemed to be part of a larger one—privation and plenty, waxing and waning—that she could glimpse only now and then, from the corner of her eye.

A shiver flooded her cheeks and her spine. Looking at the lawn, she knew suddenly how to render the letter *C*. It would need a much larger sheet of paper, maybe even a canvas—something big for the new work she had been pondering: *A* for *Armageddon*, *B* for *Bafflement*.

C would stand for *Cows*. Not one or two—but seven, the biblical number. Seven cows, fat as fat, picking their way across a frosted meadow, udders heavy with milk. While lolling up from a creek behind them, emerging out of mud and inky blackness, would come the first of their emaciated sisters.

Now this was something she could use. She felt an urge to race upstairs, begin work while her neck hairs stood on end. But even as her mind rushed, she sensed the girl standing behind her, eyes like holes, gaunt face mirrored in the window. Anna's back prickled with sick dread, though she knew what she had to do: she was from strong stock after all, women who had seen war. She just needed to spin, reach out, yank that child off balance into a tight lock. The ghost girl would kick and buck and bite, but Anna would hold on.

"It's all right," she would whisper, rocking the terrified thing in her arms. "It's all right."

CLAMS

Dear Kenneth,

*Perhaps you don't remember me, and if not I will under-
stand. It was a long time ago. More than half a century.
Who could imagine time passing so quickly?*

*I lived in a beach house near Lund. We used to go out
clamming together.*

Does that ring a bell now?

*You rolled up your pants and I said you had "city feet,"
because you made such a fuss about walking over barnacles.*

I saw you mentioned in a column in The Vancouver
Sun. *It said you were retiring after a long and esteemed
career at the bar. Not having had much of an esteemed
career myself, at first I thought you had been a bartender.
Then I saw you'd been on the board of Weyerhaeuser
Paper, which is a far cry from slinging drinks!*

I read your name and I saw you clear as life, bounding through the heather. That was how I always pictured you, when you weren't with me. Bounding up that mountain near where you came from in England, a book of poetry in your pocket. Then the memories flooded back, just like it was yesterday. The butter clams we dug up, and how a bucket of them went rotten on my porch and gave off an awful smell. How big the stars were that summer. Who could forget that? Us lying on the beach on my tartan blanket, a million stars overhead, so many of which turned out to have names. Beetlejuice was a name I remember—how about that! I still can't believe any scientist in his right mind would name a star Beetlejuice.

I suppose I ought to fill you in on my present circumstances. When Frank retired, we moved to Victoria. He died three years ago. He said he had a funny feeling in his left arm above the elbow. I said: "Funny ha-ha, or funny peculiar?" I didn't want to be callous, but those were the last words I spoke to him. He sat in the shade of the house to do the crossword and had a heart attack.

Kenneth Farraday, I do not expect you to get this letter, let alone answer it. But if you do, I'll let you know this. That summer was the happiest time of my life. I am at the Ogilvie Care Home for Seniors, if you ever find yourself "crossing the seas" to Victoria.

Sincerely, Priscilla King

KENNETH looked up from the letter. Outside his study window the lawn sloped to a border of rhododendrons with gnarled, rain-slick branches. His pride and joy. That was what Deirdre, his wife, called the rhododendrons: "Kenneth's pride and joy," suggesting a simpleness in him, he supposed, as well as misplaced priorities. In June they flamed orange and scarlet, but now they were covered in sticky buds. Beyond the hedges and cedars of the British Properties he could see the suspension rigging of the Lions Gate Bridge, and beyond that, the city's bony cliff faces.

He could hear Deirdre and his eldest daughter, Jennifer, having coffee in the kitchen. Jennifer had come to pick up their grandson after a morning with his grandmother, and the two women were murmuring about his likes and dislikes, his fussiness, his learning disability. Kenneth found his grandson difficult to be around, and blamed Jennifer for having cut his hair in bangs that emphasized his oddness.

"He's peculiar enough," Kenneth had muttered to Deirdre before Jennifer arrived, as the boy slurped milk out of his saucer. "Must he also have a peculiar haircut?"

Deirdre had shot him a look from under dark eyebrows, a look of frustration verging on fury. Verging on hatred. In menopause she had gotten used to speaking her mind with a blunt force that had shocked him, and the habit had not left her a decade and a half later.

"He's your *grandson*." She moved her mouth hard. "Show some compassion."

"It is with great compassion that I have pointed out his unfortunate haircut."

Kenneth had picked up his tray of tea and taken it to the study with the mail, leaving Deirdre with her chalkboard of tasks, machine messages from the Georgia Strait Alliance, and her simmering pot of osso bucco.

I saw you, clear as life, bounding up that mountain.

He must have told her about Urra Moor, and the image had somehow lodged in her brain, a sliver he carried too, almost painful to draw out now: running up Urra Moor in the morning, birds scattering out of the gorse, a mule deer watching his scramble. How the blood had raced through his hands and arms and shoulders. He had found a stick and waved it, infatuated with the surge of adrenalin through his body.

Funny that she—Priscilla King—had held on to this memory of a place she had never seen, while Deirdre did not even know the name Urra Moor, though he may have told her about it when he was courting her. He remembered Deirdre descending the stairs of the Vancouver Club in a lemon-chiffon

dress and gloves. Her father had been an important member. When Kenneth drove her home that
night, he had parked at Spanish Banks and pulled up
the hem of her dress, stiff as a ballerina's costume,
and touched her knee, then the birthmark high on
her left thigh. Perhaps, after that bout of rumpled
thrusting, they had lit cigarettes and he had told her
about Urra Moor. But he doubted it.

Priscilla King's handwriting was neatly formed,
the *s*'s like small sails, the *g*'s and *y*'s curled neatly
beneath each line.

I saw you clear as life.

How odd of her to write to him. The gambit of
a lonely widow. Pathetic. And what book of poetry
was she referring to? He had taken a couple of classes
in English and Philosophy while getting his degree
in forestry, before he hunkered down and focused on
law. He couldn't recall carrying a poetry book in his
pocket. What a poseur he must have been!

But now he could not stay still. He put on his
rubber boots, slid open the glass door and crossed
the lawn to the border of rhododendron, where he
snapped away twigs, then fetched a box of bone meal
from the shed, scattering handfuls among the moss.

KENNETH had met Priscilla King the summer he
worked in Lund, which was the farthest town you

could drive north to from Vancouver, along the coastal road: past Howe Sound, Gibsons, Jervis Inlet. By day Kenneth had worked in the bush with three other forestry students, Hungarian refugees who had escaped to British Columbia. Together, they measured stream heights, analyzed sediment, bushwhacked trails. He remembered lying in his bunk in the afternoon listening to them play cards. The creosote smell of the cabin, the slap of cards as he traced a knothole with his forefinger, thinking of Priscilla. It must have been a Sunday because he still remembered the anticipation in his stomach waiting for Frank to be gone, back onto his boat. Then Kenneth would wander down the beach, around three coves, to her cabin with its tarpaper roof. Always look for the warning: if she had hung a red towel on the porch rail, a rock weighing it down, then Frank was there.

She was Frank's wife, a fisherman's wife, another man's woman, and this, for Kenneth, was like an aphrodisiac: to taste, to eat of her flesh, to dive into her, to beat himself against her bones, knowing she was another man's wife, made him flush with desire as he lay on that bunk, surrounded by the smell of socks. When she moaned, he thought: *I made her moan more than Frank*. When she thrashed, he thought: *Can Frank do that?* He was stealing her, having his way illicitly. He even remembered whispering *Frank's wife* as he kissed her, noticing how she flinched. That, too, was erotic, to hurt her ever so gently. He had been young: affecting any woman had felt exhilarating and dangerous.

Only a year before, he had left North Yorkshire. Mother and Father. Tea at the rectory. He had roamed across Canada feeling like a black sheep, the bad youngest son, though in fact he was the only son, with two doting sisters, Dodie and Kitty. He had a notion about himself, which had to do with pouring himself into the Canadian vastness, submerging himself beneath massive, breathing conifers. After one lice-infested season in a logging camp near Squamish, he had amended his plans, writing to his father for money, enrolling in the University of BC's new forestry department. That was why he was in Lund with three Hungarians who drank dark beer and called to each other in their bunks at night, leaving Kenneth to speculate on the salty crack in Priscilla's ass.

Even now (under the rhododendron's waxy leaves) he remembered the fish scales on her tanned shoulders, tiny, reflective and sharp. The sand in her hair. She had been a kind of beach relic, aged, scaly, sandy. She had shown him places to lick—inner ear, belly button—and every time, because he was young and cocky, it had felt like a conquest. Only once, after they had collected clams, lying on top of her on the tartan blanket, he had been surprised to feel tears at the corners of his eyes. Gratitude? Relief? Pent-up chemical exuberance?

HE did not answer Priscilla King's letter.

Instead he waited for a month, and then he lied to Deirdre, telling her he would be lunching with the Weyerhaeuser advisory committee, then going to the club. She would not be home until late; she had her Georgia Strait Alliance board meeting. Then Kenneth took the ferry to Victoria.

He found a spot by the window, placing his coat and scarf on the seat beside him. They passed the tip of a Gulf island, a red-painted government wharf. Sights like this must have been part of Priscilla's life, for years and years, as she and Frank returned from fishing on his seiner. And now a voice began to intone, a rocking cadence beneath the engine's hum:

And therefore I have sailed the seas and come
To the holy city of Byzantium.

And then, almost like his father's voice, it was so fever-sharp:

An aged man is but a paltry thing,
A tattered coat upon a stick, unless
Soul clap its hands and sing, and louder sing
For every tatter in its mortal dress—

Where had these voices been? Gone, that was all.

CLAMMING: you place your socks inside your shoes and put them on a rock above the high-tide mark. She looks at your feet, which have never seen a day's sun, and she says, "Time to toughen those tootsies, Kenneth."

And you say, "Alliteration, Priscilla."

She smiles radiantly, exposing an incisor inexpertly filled with silver.

"You don't know what alliteration is, do you, Priscilla?"

She walks down the beach, not caring.

You call, "Priscilla prances precisely over provocative pebbles," and she turns and you know you will lie on top of her tonight, her in all her perplexity and supplicant moaning, her womanly needs.

Come on, Kenneth. I'm going to teach you to catch clams.

I thought they just lay in their shells, and you scooped them up.

———

AFTER the clamming, he'd gone for a night swim then come up the beach, wrapped in a towel. She was on the blanket, crying. He threw himself down beside her.

"Prissy. You're a mess."

"Maybe I'll kill myself," she said, conversationally. "I have pills. The doctor gave them to me."

"Are you crazy?"

"Maybe I am." She lit a cigarette, blew smoke toward the scrim of stars. "You leave. You go to your university. I stay."

He kissed the salty tears from her temple, feeling both sorry for her and distanced, in another land, walking among other people, discussing Plato and Locke, discussing Milton.

After that summer, for years, if he saw a seiner crossing the Strait, the words *Frank's wife* would flit through his mind, along with the taste of sex in the setting sun—and that was it.

HE stood outside the Ogilvie Care Home for Seniors, a concrete building of pallid mauve, like cold skin. The glass doors slid open as a nurse wheeled a man into the sunlight. The man clutched a cane, the end propped on the chair's footrest. He wore leather slippers like Kenneth's slippers at home. The doors closed, muffled by a thousand brushes hidden in the door sockets. From down by the seawall a child's voice rose: *I want a bagel, I want a bagel, I want a bagel!* A seaplane scudded across the bay. Kenneth stepped on the automatic-door rug, and the doors hissed open, withdrawing into their hairy keeps.

The lobby tiles had been buffed to a mirrorlike brilliance, reflecting the penumbra of Kenneth's white hair. By the window a cleaning woman patiently ministered to a collection of tropical plants, caressing a dampened paper towel over each broad leaf. Solitary figures in wheelchairs had been set out here and there, deployed, Kenneth thought, like chess pieces. He shivered as he made his way to the check-in desk. The nurse looked up, visible pores on her nose. A crucifix dangled between her large breasts. Lebanese, she might be, or Spanish.

"Is there a Priscilla King here?"

"Who's visiting?"

"A friend."

The nurse glanced at his hat, now in his hand, and at his jacket and tie, then typed on a keypad and checked the computer screen. "She's had a fall. She's upstairs now. Room 319. Come." A single word, as though to a child.

Kenneth followed her buttocks down the corridor to the elevator. They went up to the third floor, which had walls the colour of a pool, long-legged insects reflected in wobbly patterns through glass. He heard the sigh of recirculating air.

The nurse paused before a door, knocked on it briskly and then pushed it open.

"Prissy, you've got a friend to see you."

She held the door. Kenneth entered.

Two women were parked in parallel beds. The woman in the far bed had frizzy hair around her ears, but the top of her head was bald like one of the Three Stooges. Moe? Curly? Kenneth had never known which stooge was which.

The woman in the second, closer, bed was Priscilla.

She shifted her head with a single heavy motion and fixed Kenneth with her gaze. She was over eighty—her hair had turned white, her face had weathered, lines deepening, cheeks sinking, sultry lips cracking—but she was still Priscilla, and he felt an urge to say, *You haven't changed*, because she hadn't, not really. The years on Frank's boat had merely crystallized her, like a piece of candied ginger.

Kenneth advanced to the bedside. "Hello, Priscilla," he said softly. "I'm Kenneth Farraday."

"Who?" She squinted at him.

"It's me. Kenneth. You wrote me a letter."

She took out her hearing aid, gave him a complicit smile, flicked the plastic sound piece and then replaced it in her ear. "I dropped the damned thing in the maple syrup this morning," she said. "Now, come again: Who did you say you were? Because I want you to know one thing, I pay my taxes." She turned to her companion in the next bed to share this piece of drollery, but the other woman had fallen asleep. Priscilla went through the elaborate head motion again, and fixed her gaze on Kenneth. She had caught hold of the edge of the bedsheet.

"You wrote to me," he said.

"Now why would I do that?"

He found himself blushing. "I knew you a long time ago. I'm *Kenneth*, Priscilla."

A pause. A beat. He watched the message pass in through the syrup-covered hearing aid, along the crotchety synapses, and into the pupils of Priscilla's eyes.

IN the lobby a woman in a wheelchair raised a clawed hand to waylay him in his passage across the sea of tiles, but Kenneth kept moving, through the sliding doors, past the hideous fuchsia hanging in their baskets, along the seawall. Two Native women lay on the grass eating fried chicken from a paper bucket. Let them. What did he care?

He found a bench, sat and looked at his watch. The back of his hand was drained of colour. He had two hours until his ferry left the harbour. If he went now, he could wash his hands in the bathroom of the Empress hotel, then eat curry at the Bengal Lounge, before driving back to the ferry. But he stayed where he was.

After Kenneth had said his name, Priscilla had searched his face, just as though she were digging in the sand, scrabbling with her fingers, clawing to see one vestige, one aspect of the Kenneth she had known, before settling again on his pupils.

"You see. It's me."

She made a sound like *youch*, or *ouch*. "You can't be."

He answered before he could help himself. "Why can't I be?"

"You're nothing like him."

"I'm older. *We're* older."

She looked from his face to his hands, then shook her head angrily. "You remind me of an egg." Oh, the look on her face as she said those words, a kind of practical malevolence, as though she knew exactly what she was doing.

At that moment the nurse bustled in to give Priscilla a pill. She told Kenneth he could sit, and he sat. When the nurse was gone, he spoke again.

"I got your letter. I thought I'd pay you a visit."

"You did, did you?"

"You invited me."

"I gave the letter to the nurse. I didn't think she had mailed it."

"Well, she did."

Sunshine attached itself to the slats of the blinds, lighting each edge to brilliance. When he glanced back, Priscilla was looking at him with fascinated disgust. And why? What warranted this reaction? He smelled of aftershave, no doubt, and he was elderly (though not as old as she was). He had on a finely cut jacket, and a scarf, and carried a hat with a small feather in the ribbon.

She said, "Do you miss him?"

"Who?"

"Kenneth."

Now he was angry.

She said, "I miss him."

"*Who* do you miss, Priscilla?"

She paused, and then gave him a crafty smirk. "Frank," she said.

He sat for another minute, and then he told her he must go. As he opened the door, he heard her say to the woman in the next bed, "That's a real cock-of-the-block. A puffed-up bird, that one."

Now Kenneth looked out at the bay. Buildings rippled and broke in the water.

How long before Priscilla forgot that he had visited—before the boy, Kenneth, returned to her? The reader of poetry. The leaper of gorse bushes. A sleep, a wakening, and then he'd be back. In fact, Kenneth-the-boy might have slipped from the room a second before Kenneth arrived, and danced back in the side door a second after the old cock-of-the-block took his hat and departed. Fury prickled Kenneth's back. The old bird. The old, dried-up bird with her brittle bones, hoary toes, cracked skin. Why should she have such access to his boyhood self when Kenneth himself had nothing?

He got up and walked to the parking lot. No curry this time. He would drive to the ferry, and he would never cross the Strait again. Priscilla had had her revenge. The great karmic wheel of time (something Deirdre believed in) had spun round and now she, Priscilla, had finished on top. One part of her mind was addled, there was no question of that, but another part, using senility as a cover, had slithered across the floor, crafty as a snake, and lashed out.

Do you miss him?

HIS car went over the ramp with a thump, into the belly of the boat. Squeezing out through his door, he found himself face to face with a teenage boy holding a dog on a leash. "Get that thing away from me," Kenneth said.

Upstairs he found a seat by the window. Children on the deck were playing at being blown back, coats like sails. Behind him a Punjabi family ate spiced rice and fried meat from plastic containers. Bracelets jingled as the mother took out food.

One of the children outside had a red coat, the same shade as the towel that Priscilla used to set on the porch railing, a rock weighing it down. Priscilla who now lay in bed like a dried-up bird. He pictured red pubic hair beneath the hospital gown, a softened belly, bones so frail you could break them just by lying on top of her. And the look on her face—the spite and satisfaction as she had insulted him. He stood and walked down the aisle, past the ferry takeout restaurant. Something was moving in him. Something old. Something strange.

From what I've tasted of desire
I hold with those who favor fire.

Oh, Prissy, he almost moaned. *You got me good. You got me by the short and curlies this time.* But here he stopped short, making a woman behind him spill her coffee. She scowled as she passed him, but he shook his head, because it had come to him. The solution, that was all. The very solution to his problem.

He would return. Lying to Deirdre, lying and

sneaking, driving to the ferry, crossing the Holy Sea on his mission. And such a mission it would be. And who could say, who could slice it fine enough to say if it would be a mission of contrition or revenge?

"It's me," he will say, standing by the bed, once every month, like clockwork.

Hat. Overcoat. Gloves. Cravat. Umbrella.

"It's me," he will positively purr.

She will turn her head with that rolling gesture. "Who?" Mouth puckered in fear.

"Kenneth."

"No!"

"Yes!"

Priscilla will edge back, grasping the blanket, buzzing, if strength allows, for the nurse. ("Isn't it sweet," the nurse will say, "how he visits so regularly?") Then he will meet Priscilla's eyes, forcing her to see him, prying open her mind to expose those last spots that hold the other Kenneth, sucking them out like buttery clam meat.

THE COFFIN STORY

Pa aged. It seemed only yesterday that he had been a despot, striking Jackie across the palms with the wooden ruler he kept on a nail by the kitchen door. He never used the metal ruler—he was firm but fair, Mums always said, though to Jackie, at seven, Pa was a whirlwind of fury, a sensation of sickness at the pit of his stomach. But Pa aged. He altered. So that to Jackie, heading now into his own middle years, Pa seemed to have stepped right out of his skin, transforming in a single, shimmering second from a monster of punishment to a bewildered gentleman in sheepskin slippers and a tartan robe.

They lived in the Town of Ardrossan on the Firth of Clyde. For fifty-six years Pa had dispensed four-inch nails and six-inch nails, sheet metal and plungers from behind the marble counter of

Hobbes' Ironmongery. But eventually Pa retired, and Mums died, and Jackie, urged on by his wife, Karen, changed the name of the shop to Hobbes' Do-It-Yourself. Together they brought in fluorescent light bulbs and toaster ovens and hand-held blenders.

Pa lived above the shop, and on days when things were quiet, Jackie could hear his father walking around upstairs, making the beams creak. Though he was a spare man, he had a heavy way of walking. Jackie could tell when Pa was making tea, when he was frying his lunch, and when he had settled in the leather chair by the window to read his newspaper.

Pa made two trips outside each day: to the newsagent in the morning, to collect his paper, and to the pier in the afternoon. He could tell what each ship's freight was by the height of its hull, and knew at a glance whether it was built on the Clyde. The rest of the time Pa sat in his chair by the window, where he had an excellent view of people beneath. He knew who had entered the chemist's, and when the delivery girl would bike up the hill, and that Jackie's neighbours, the ones with the new car, had picked up a large package from the butcher's.

At six Jackie let down the blinds of his shop. The bell tinkled as he flipped the sign to "Closed," then he crossed quickly to the pub down the street, the

Hole in the Wa'. He downed a pint and then headed back across the road. He knew Pa was watching him. The top of Jackie's bald head glowed, he knew, and the tips of his ears turned red, so strange and fierce did it feel to have his father looking down at him, though it happened every night.

Jackie unlocked the door on the street and climbed the stairs. They were extremely narrow and at least a hundred years old. Ten or twelve steps up, they turned abruptly at a narrow landing. The walls smelled of ancient, salty limestone.

Jackie let himself in through the kitchen, with its felted pattern of black peonies. Pa sat by the window in the front room.

"Stepped across to the pub," Jackie said.

"I saw."

Jackie settled in the chair opposite. It had a view of the gasworks and the foundry. Between them a slash of blue, which was the Firth of Clyde.

"But tell me, Pa, what happened here today?"

Beneath his wild, unruly eyebrows, Pa squinted with malice. "That Sinnett boy, I caught him trying to pry the lock from Mary Clough's bicycle. He didn't know I could see him, tinkering like a thief. I threw a book at him, clear across the road."

"You didn't."

"Just about beaned him. 'I'll report you,' I told

him—but I wanted you to come sooner. The book sat there all day."

"Is it still out there?" The delivery bike stood where it always did, chained to the pole. "I can't see it, Pa."

"It fell behind that car."

"That one there?" Jackie pointed to a Mini a full ten feet from the bicycle.

Pa reached for his tobacco and began to stuff his pipe.

"What book was it, Pa?"

"One of your mother's."

But all of the books had been Jackie's mother's. It was an easy sort of answer, and made Jackie think his father might have made the story up, just to have something to tell.

The setting sun spread a pink flush across the whitewashed walls of the chemist's shop.

"I've got a problem for you," Pa said now, by way of changing the subject. "A conundrum." He lit a match and sucked on his pipe.

Jackie looked up warily. When Jackie was younger, Pa had often scoffed at his slowness in handling tools. He remembered his father's legs sticking out from beneath the sink, voice muffled: *Not the monkey wrench, you dolt—the number two clamp.* In such situations, Mums intervened, a flutter of white cloth, the smell of Jergens, puffy feet padding across the linoleum.

The sun lowered another eighth of an inch. The room was cooler.

"Go on," Jackie said.

"You won't be able to solve it."

"Give me a try." He lit a cigarette.

"Better pour us a drink."

Jackie got the bottle from the cupboard, poured out two glasses and set them on the round table between the two chairs. "Now go on. A conundrum, you said."

"A veritable conundrum."

Pa took a sip, gasping appreciation for the burning in his throat, and then set the glass down. "I went out walking today," he said. "Decided to visit Princes Street. Monroe and Sons."

Jackie felt his stomach tense.

"Funeral home. In my day they were called undertakers, but that's all changed. It's a fancy establishment now, coffins laid out like sports cars. The younger Monroe boy was there. He owns the place with his brother. Helpful fellow."

"I'm glad, Pa."

"I must have spent an hour with him. His name's Nick. His brother's Bob.

"That's right—I went to school with them."

"I decided to get a simple vessel. 'Universal,' it's called. White ash, brushed-iron hinges, lined in satin. Coffin shaped. Not one of those caskets."

Jackie sighed. Even when Pa was a much younger man, in his forties, he would talk like this, waxing lugubrious about getting old, as though he were the only person who would ever experience the pattern of aging. *I'm old*, he would groan at the supper table, *so old, Margy*. To which Mums would say, *Nonsense, George, you're not so old*. Jackie, sitting between them, staring at the oilcloth, longed to meet his father's eyes: *You're ancient*, he wanted to spit, but he kept his head down and ate his peas.

"That's good to be prepared. Though, it could be years yet."

"But here's my dilemma. Nick Monroe says to me, 'Where do you want to be laid out?' He says I can be laid out in 'the home'—that's the room they have at the funeral place. But I won't have it."

"Perhaps the sitting room at our house. Karen—"

"I told him I'll be laid out here. Right here in this room. He and Bob Monroe will bring the coffin up and set it out. I suppose they'll need a table of some sort. I'll be laid out with all the rigmarole for three days, and there'll be a crying and a wringing of hands, and a general mourning will run up and down the land. The bells will ring and the women will wail."

"Pa!"

"Then they'll carry my coffin in state down the Princes Street to the Barony Church, and then on to the cemetery, digging a hole beside Mums. But now—and here's my conundrum." He set down his pipe and rubbed his palms together. "You've seen the stairs."

"What stairs?"

"The ones you use every day, man. For God's sake, don't be a dolt. Well, here's the thing—the coffin will never fit around that narrow bend at the landing. It's too tight a spot." With an air of triumph he sat back, looking at Jackie from beneath his white eyebrows.

"Pa," said Jackie gently. "You may need to get a slimmer casket."

"That's their thinnest model."

"Should I telephone the Monroes?"

"Don't you think of it."

"They're professionals, Pa. They'll figure it out."

"They go by the book. I've got the dimensions right here." He took a folded piece of paper from his jacket pocket. On it he had pencilled measurements of coffin, door with frame, door without frame, hallway and landing. "I've been thinking about this all afternoon," Pa said. "And I can't find a solution, except perhaps to set up a pulley system from the window, lower the coffin in a canvas sling. It won't be easy. And it would cost."

"No cost would be too much."

"I've paid my way. Left you without debt. Shop in good shape."

"Of course, Pa." Jackie suspected Pa knew about the bank loan, and the purchase of fifty Cuisinart food processors, which had not sold well. "What ships came in today?"

"Three freighters and the *Penny Loonan.*"

"Clyde built?"

"Monrovian flags. Hulls looked Polish, but don't distract me. I tell you, we have a problem. A rare problem."

Pa had gotten himself into a lather, and Jackie could do nothing to distract him. So they sat together and smoked and talked about the problem until Midge came in to cook Pa's dinner.

Then Jackie left, seven o'clock sharp, back to Karen and his daughter, Elaine, who was sixteen, studying for her exams and smoking a lot of pot. He wondered which side of Elaine he would see tonight: drugged, sleepy, feeding herself in a frenzy, or bent over her books at the kitchen counter. As he walked up the hill he thought about the debt, and Karen's plans for curtains in the sitting room. She would want him to choose from the samples. He remembered the stairwell leading from Pa's apartment, the smell of salt rising from the walls. Pa's right, Jackie thought, they'll never get a coffin down those narrow stairs.

NOW every time Jackie stepped in, his father brought it up. *I've been ruminating,* he would say, *about this issue of the coffin.* Or, *I've been wondering. I've been thinking.* For the forty-five minutes that Jackie and his father sat together, they would talk it through.

One day Jackie brought a drawing he had done on the back of an envelope. He had done it to scale in the quiet of the afternoon, when he should have been tackling the books. "I think," he said, as soon as he was seated with his cigarette going, "you'll appreciate the ease of the solution."

"Is it elegant?"

"It is."

"I like a little elegance. Give it here."

Jackie handed the envelope to his father, who laid it flat on the small table between them. The answer Jackie had come up with *was* elegant—it required only a boat hook drilled into the beam at the top of the stairwell, then a lifting of the coffin's head at the top door, a spin of the thing at the landing. All this he'd written out neatly, with arrows showing degrees of spin and angles of lift.

"They'll carry me out standing, will they?" Pa gave a huff, which turned to a cough, which became the hacking of brown stuff into his pocket handkerchief.

Jackie got water from the kitchen tap. When he returned, his father said: "You've got your mum's good handwriting, haven't you."

Jackie said nothing. He felt praised to the roots of his hair.

"So what do you think, Pa?"

"About what?" Pa seemed bewildered, then glanced down at the envelope and took a breath. "Just about, lad," Pa said. "But if you tip me on the vertical, the coffin will hit the ceiling. As for the door jamb—even taking the hinges off won't do the trick. I think we're better off thinking about the window. I can tell you, this thing is harder than it looks."

THAT night Jackie dreamed of the stairwell, his father standing at the top. He held his cane and wore a satin robe and a fur cap on his head. Jackie was below, beside a copper urn that had held a fern in his childhood house, and there were other things jamming up the hallway too: a coat rack full of overcoats and ski jackets, some of Elaine's CDs, their cases smashed, and several Cuisinarts from the hardware store. Jackie mounted the stairs to take Pa's elbow, but Pa lashed out at him with his cane. *Stay back or I'll brain you,* he hissed.

"If we could convince him to stay here," Jackie said to Karen the next morning, "we wouldn't have this problem."

Karen spun to look at him. "You know he won't move."

Karen still smarted from things Pa had said years ago about her family, though they were bricklayers at Saltcoats and only one of them—a distant uncle—had ended up in jail for a cheque kiting scheme. They were nothing for Pa to look down on. She got three hard-boiled eggs and set them out in red egg cups. The egg for Elaine looked hopeful, though they both knew that Elaine would not emerge from the bathroom for another twenty minutes, and probably would not eat the egg because she was watching her weight.

"I don't understand," Karen said, "how two grown men can go on like this, talking about a coffin."

"Oh, I don't know."

"It's morbid, Jackie, that's what it is. Morbid— plain and simple."

PA did die. It was Midge, coming up to fry his lunch, who discovered him. She ran for Jackie, who was measuring copper wire. Jackie sprinted from the shop and up the stairs. There was Pa, in his chair, by the window. His eyes were open but unseeing, and no breath moved his chest. It all seemed to Jackie like a last trick on Pa's part. He could not shake this idea even as he told Midge to call the doctor.

Jackie stepped down the road and turned onto Princes Street, where, for the first time, he entered the Monroe funeral home. He rang the bell. Nick Monroe came from the back—the coffin showroom, no doubt. He was tall and lean and younger than Jackie: a track star, Jackie remembered now, good at the dash. His brother, Bob, who appeared and stood beside Nick, had been good at swimming. Small dark heads. Noses like clothes pegs.

"My father," Jackie said. "He's gone."

Jackie felt almost elated by the oddness of it, the combination of portentous dignity and hollow strangeness in the act of saying, *He's gone*—as though the old man had really done it this time, setting them on a course of preposterous mischief. Underneath were darker currents, logs piling up in a river. Jackie's cheeks felt moist and cold, as if he had walked through fog.

The brothers seemed perturbed. Bereavement was mentioned. A framework for grieving. Assistance.

"I don't care about all that," Jackie said, picking up on why his father had set against these brothers. "Just bring the coffin," he said.

The brothers consulted a dossier. They told him that his father's wishes would be respected, but that prior to the visitation his father's body must be brought to the funeral home for care. They would carry him on a stretcher, covered in a funereal cloth.

"Oh no you bloody don't," said Jackie. "He may need some fixing up here, prior to visitation, but he doesn't leave that room except he's in that coffin. Those were his wishes, plain as plain, though the stairwell is a tight one, as you'll see for yourselves."

How strange these words were, sung out by himself alone, without the force of his father's will to back him. But they were enough. The Monroe brothers got the coffin, the Universal, with its metal fittings and white ash, and they carried it behind Jackie up Princes Street, past the Hole in the Wa' pub, to the door to Pa's rooms. Jackie went ahead of them up the stairs, poured himself a drink and sat down across from his father. He heard scraping and banging and swearing coming from the landing, then the Monroes emerged, sweating furiously. They laid the coffin, lidless, on the front room floor.

"Now mind, that lid must be hinged on tight when you leave."

They looked at him as though he were mad, and the elder Monroe put a hand on the other's elbow. Jackie narrowed his eyes with spite and turned back to his drink.

The two brothers set about their work, reattaching the lid, wiping the edging with a cloth. The satin caught the light from the casement and glowed, showing sheens of grey hidden in the nap. Pa was taken from his robe, and his slippers were exchanged for shoes and socks. As Nick Monroe knelt, pulling a sock over Pa's hoary toenails, the certainty in Jackie washed out. They placed Pa in the coffin, then asked Jackie if he wanted a time alone with the deceased, but Jackie shook his head.

They heaved up the coffin.

At the kitchen door it wedged fast, and Jackie let out a single, painful sigh. They moved back into the kitchen, turned the coffin onto what must have been less than a twenty-degree angle, and then they went at the door again, wiggling, adjusting for hinges, for girth. Through it slid.

Jackie heard their voices rising from the landing, advising each other to stay above the banister, to hold the coffin higher, to give a twist. "Just about," he heard Nick Monroe say. "Easy now." Then they were out, carrying the coffin down Princes Street toward the funeral home.

The entire departure took less than seven minutes.

IN the years to come, Jackie told the coffin story half a dozen times at the pub, but it never came out right.

People didn't understand. Once someone told him he shouldn't make fun of his old man. Let him rest in peace, they said, which made no sense at all. Another time the conversation drifted to the narrowness of stairwells, how the new houses were better than the older ones, for exactly that reason. Once his daughter, Elaine, who was older now, and sweeter, put a hand on his arm. "It's a lovely story, Dad," she said. "And wouldn't Pa have been shocked to see how easy his coffin went round the corner, after all that worrying. He should have been there, eh, Dad?" But of course that was not the point either.

Karen worked the counter every day now, and Elaine, who had been to business school in Glasgow, managed the books so effectively, and got along so well with her mother, that Jackie sometimes didn't go to the shop until mid-afternoon. Elaine had come up with all sorts of ideas for making the place more up to date, even changing the name back to Hobbes' Ironmongery, which did seem to attract the upscale clients looking for vintage doorknobs, and claw feet for their bathtubs.

Jackie would read the paper in the sunroom, then walk from the suburbs to Princes Street, then along to the docks. He noted the freighters, trying to guess which were Clyde built. Staring out at the seagulls circling the fish boats, he remembered the days bent over the coffin drawings. His father so fierce, jubilant even, as though he would cheat death with his coffin ploy. Was that it? Not quite. There was something else at the heart of the story, some lesson that Jackie felt he almost understood.

He remembered the sun falling slantwise through the casement, both of them bent over the drawing, studying it carefully. The quiet fascination, motes of dust floating above the carpet. Ice melting in a glass. That his father would have troubled himself like this, poring over each of Jackie's drawings, showing him how to face seaward, if you could call it that, face into the wind, like a sea captain facing into a gale, while never letting on how dire it was, this came to Jackie to seem extraordinary.

And so, in the end, the coffin story wasn't something others needed to understand. Jackie understood it. And it gave his days a quiet satisfaction, turning from the dock, walking back up the street past the pub and pork butchers, toward the shop. The old man was right, Jackie thought, grimly pleased to have arrived at this place, holding the puzzle in his own hands now. The whole damned thing is harder than it looks.

THE WIND

Shulamith leaned across the kitchen table and gazed into her friend Nancy's eyes. Nancy wondered if Shulamith intended to speak at all. She seemed as though she might just sit there, yogically balanced on her erect spine.

"I'm afraid," Shulamith said at last. "Really afraid."

"Of what? Tell me."

"You know, I'm afraid to even talk about it. I don't want to make it more real."

"You've got to talk it through," Nancy said. "Besides, why did I come all this way if you don't want to tell me?"

Shulamith gave Nancy a piercing look of sorrow, and then pulled back her ferocious golden and red curls. God, thought Nancy, Shulamith could make any state look enviable. Even severe distress. Even heartbreak. Still, Nancy was excited to hear what Shulamith's dilemma was. Her belly tightened, and the light through the kitchen window actually altered. The sun must have gone behind a cloud then reappeared, revamped, ready for action.

They were in Shulamith's kitchen on Galiano Island. Nancy had arrived several days early for their climate change meeting because Shulamith had told her on the phone that she needed help. Fine. Nancy was good at helping. Now here they were sipping Body & Soul tea from bumpily glazed island mugs— the table laid with honey pot, dipper stick, cream in a little pitcher shaped like a cow.

"All right," said Shulamith. "It's Ramsey."

Ramsey was Shulamith's five-year-old son. Nancy felt a surge of disappointment.

Shulamith must have caught it, because she reached for the honey pot and said, "You thought it was going to be about Charlie."

"Not necessarily." Nancy's heart was beating faster, as it always did at the mention of Charlie.

"It's usually Charlie—let's face it."

Charlie was Shulamith's husband. He was part Cherokee, with a shaved head, broad shoulders, a thin waist, and a habit of laughing softly at Nancy's jokes. He was also the source of numerous infidelities, painstakingly related at this same table.

"No. This time it's Ramsey. My baby." Shulamith

tucked one foot up on the chair, under her bum, an expert gesture practised, Nancy thought, since Grade Four: how the cool girls used to sit as they coloured with their peacock and magenta crayons.

"So what is it? What's happened?"

"I'm afraid you'll laugh."

"Why on earth would I laugh—you're obviously upset. Besides, I never laugh where Ramsey's concerned."

A pause. Then Shulamith said: "He's afraid to go outside."

"You're serious."

"I'm serious."

The two women looked at each other, and then they both burst out laughing, though Shulamith had a stricken look in her eyes, and Nancy's laugh sounded a bit too much like a hoot of derision. It was just so ironic. Shulamith and Charlie had moved to this island so that Ramsey could run across shell beaches, hardening the soles of his bare feet, swim naked at night in the phosphorescence. Be a wild child. The ferry ride complicated Shulamith's work, but Nancy, who was on the personnel committee of their organization, had backed her up. (Charlie, a guitar maker, didn't have to explain why he wanted to live on an island. Guitar makers *always* wanted to live on islands.)

"They're all coming," Shulamith said. "The whole campaign team. And they'll be like, 'Let's go kayaking,' or 'Let's go hike Bodega Ridge,' and Ramsey will start crying, and I'll have to look at them and say, 'Actually, we don't go outside anymore—my son hates nature.'"

"Who cares what they say?"

"I know. You're right. It's just that they're always looking for ways to poke holes in me."

"No, they're not."

"Anyway, you're right: it's not the point. Not close to the point."

Shulamith sat up tall. She was five foot ten, and when she closed her eyes and swayed slightly, she was like a cobra about to strike. "The real point is— what is going on inside Ramsey?"

"You must have talked to him."

"He won't say."

"What about that cougar you told me about. Do you think he heard about that?"

A cougar had recently swum across from Vancouver Island and killed three sheep, but Shulamith sloughed that off: "If it was the cougar we'd all be fine. I mean *everyone's* afraid of a cougar. They're fucking deadly. But that cougar is long gone. It's something else."

Again Shulamith closed her eyes, the better to

pick up the vibrational meaning of her son's fear. She said, "I sometimes wonder if he's got it from us. We're always talking about the earth—the ice cap melting, polar bears dying, trees getting hit with spruce beetles. It's all so awful, twenty-four seven. And I was so sad after the Copenhagen Summit, I think I may—we may—have instilled our fear in him. And so now, he just doesn't want to look at nature at all. It frightens him because everything's sick."

"Like being at the bedside of a dying aunt," Nancy offered.

"Exactly. You know, I have to take the car to pick him up after school. If I so much as tell him we're walking, he throws himself onto the floor and rolls up in a ball. Once, after he calmed down, he went to the schoolhouse door and opened it a crack and listened. Just stood and listened. It was the eeriest thing."

Nancy could picture Ramsey clutching the door handle, his virgin-rain-forest curls falling to his shoulders. They had never been touched by scissors. His lips were absurdly kissable, like Marilyn Monroe lips, and his soft, brown cheeks—if you laid your own cheek against them they were cool and plump, though lately Nancy had noticed the beginning of his thinner, boy's face emerging out of the preschooler's roundness.

"What was he listening for?"

"I don't know. There's so much about the weather that's so *wrong* now. Toxins. Storms caused by climate change." Shulamith shook her head. "Can you pick him up today, after school? Maybe you can find out what's going on. He loves his auntie Nan. Just make sure to take the car."

"I'll walk."

"No way. He won't go."

"I'll be fine. I have my ways."

Shulamith reached out and placed both her hands over Nancy's. "You really are my best friend, you know," she said. "I can't talk to Charlie about it at all. He just thinks I'm to blame for fussing too much. Or getting too sad about the planet. But I don't think—"

"You're not to blame, Shulamith. Really."

Shulamith nodded, but she looked as though she were drowning, and it was up to Nancy— blond, cheerful Nancy—to save her. Nancy with her dykishly cut hair, though she wasn't a dyke, and her tattered T-shirt and jeans. If she were fifteen pounds lighter she would be really good looking, that was what people said, good looking in a Doris Day kind of way. Freckles and good cheer. But she wasn't fifteen pounds lighter.

"It's nothing you've done," Nancy said adamantly, "don't worry."

———

OF course Shulamith was to blame, Nancy thought a few minutes later, as she took the trail to the guest house. Shulamith had folded and contorted Ramsey, not exactly into her own image—that would be too simple a formula—but she had kneaded and pressed him so that he conformed to the negative space around her. Ever since Copenhagen, Shulamith had been depressed. She was caught (she had said it more than once, in tears, on the telephone) in a world that felt hopeless. She had done her diva-like all at the summit, accosting the first minister of China at a cocktail party, this strikingly beautiful, huge-haired woman suddenly turning to ask what he meant by not signing the protocol, then the next day hanging a banner from a bridge: *Stop the Burning of the Earth*. Banners. Cocktails. She had been gone for a month. She had fought, worked, cried, and now (this is what she had told Nancy on the telephone) she felt gutted.

Shulamith and Charlie lived on a bluff overlooking Trincomali Channel, in a forest of big-leaf maple, arbutus and second-growth cedar. In spring the maple trees put out curls of electric newness, but now the leaves were yellow, rustling above Nancy's head, a whooshing that carried from tree to tree down the bluff, where it was picked up by the cedar in another, darker register.

At the guest house Nancy changed into her rain shell and runners. The cabin smelled of woodsmoke. A bed nook covered by a Hudson's Bay blanket had windows on three sides made of horizontal French doors, so that in bed, in the rain, you could look out at the forest through walls of paned glass. Charlie had done that. He had made glass walls out of scrounged doors. Nancy transferred her cigarettes from her purse to her rain shell, lit one, took a few puffs, then lifted the lid of the wood stove and threw it in.

Dear God. Poor Ramsey, Nancy thought, as she closed the driftwood latch of the guest house and started down the trail toward the island school. Friable leaves crunched under her feet. She pictured Shulamith holding the telephone close, whispering the words of the scourge, *timber beetle, toxic waste, polar melt,* trying to keep this burden from Ramsey, just the way you might try to protect a child from the knowledge of death itself, only to have it accumulate in the shadows, a pattern of grainy darkness.

SHULAMITH and Nancy's friendship had started ten years before, in the Temagami Wilderness Committee: they had been clasped side by side (bike locks and industrial-strength chain) to the wheel shaft of a logging truck. TV reporters turned out, and Shulamith managed to twist her body to face the cameras, assuming a praying mantis position, doing interview after interview about the desecration of the forests. In between Nancy had amused Shulamith with stories of her dog.

They both went on to work for the International Campaign against Climate Change (Nancy drawn to administration; Shulamith scaling the heights of campaign stardom), and they both moved to the west coast. When Shulamith got pregnant, everyone wondered what sort of mother she'd be. "Can you picture it?" Nancy said. "She'll be in jail, and she'll suddenly think, 'Oh fuck, my baby!'" They would have to hire a new admin person: post-protest baby finder. But Shulamith surprised them again. She strained organic baby food and expressed milk before every demonstration. She spoke from the stage with the baby strapped to her chest. Nancy admired Shulamith for proving them wrong, but she couldn't help but feel, whenever she spent any time with Shulamith, that a brush fire was being set in her own body. Did they always have to talk about Shulamith's problems, her difficult marriage, the baby's sleep patterns? But it was more than that. Shulamith was just so *big*—so full of the belief that she was the centre of her own drama. Sometimes, when they spoke about the planet, it was as though they were actually talking about Shulamith. That was how big she was. The forests were her red-gold hair. The mountains were her copious, wobbling breasts. The fishy waters were the gorge between her thighs.

NANCY stepped from the forest path onto the gravel shoulder of the road and almost bumped into Charlie.

"Wow. Nancy."

"Charlie."

"Man. You startled me."

"I didn't mean to leap out at you."

"You didn't. I was lost in thought."

He gave off the powerful rays she associated with him, a sheen of attractiveness, like shafts of light from a Renaissance angel. But what got her were his eyes. She felt the jolt of recognition as their eyes met: like looking into the eyes of an incredibly well-known-to-you dog. Or meeting your own eyes in the mirror. And then that half-smile on his lips as he looked away, because he had felt it too.

But if he felt it, how could he live without it?

He said: "So you're here."

Again, the eyes. The jolt.

"I'm here."

"Has Shulamith put you in charge of the pickup?"

"Yeah."

"Ramsey's been acting out."

"What's it all about?"

He scratched at the gravel with the toe of his running shoe. "Shulamith is overcomplicating things, but I have a feeling you'll figure it out."

"Don't be too sure."

"Oh, you will." He shook his head, amazed by her: that was what that look said. Then he placed his hands on her shoulders. A surge of electricity ran down her spine, into her vagina, a tweaking action, like tightening a screw. He stepped forward and enfolded her. He was wearing a Cowichan sweater. He smelled of sheep lanolin. "Can I see you tonight?" he murmured into her hair. "Just to talk?"

She wanted to memorize the details for later, but it was an onslaught, like collecting rocks and being hit by a slide. She even heard herself think: *How will I ever sort all these pieces?* She felt his lips at her ear, hot breath against the whorls, his tongue. Then he stepped back.

"I'm sorry, Nancy."

"It's okay."

"We said we wouldn't do this."

You said, she thought. *You said.* "Yes, you can come," she said. "But just to talk."

"To talk."

"That's right."

He shook his head, looking amazed all over again, and then he checked his watch. It was an involuntary gesture, and when he noticed she had caught it, he smiled ruefully, already regretting it, as he clearly regretted much else. He hugged her again, a brotherly hug this time, and then they parted, Charlie up the wooded trail, Nancy along the ocean road to the school.

RAMSEY was in the schoolhouse, drawing a dog on the computer. When Nancy tapped him on the shoulder, he seemed not to notice, then looked up and realized it was her. He called out *Nancy, Nancy, Nancy* and threw himself into her arms. He was heavier, and Nancy was astonished, all over again, at how beautiful he was. She smelled him like a rose: smelled his scalp, dirty and sandy. *Could I love you any more than this?* Nancy thought. But what she said was, "I have chocolate."

"What kind?"

"You'll see. Put your coat on."

His eyes darted to the window. A look of fear.

"Hey—go quick," she said. "They're M&M's."

That worked. He went to his cubby and found his running shoes and Velcro'd them on, then pulled on his fleece and put on his Spider-Man backpack.

The whole place smelled of melted wax. The teacher, wiping her hands on a paper towel, came toward Nancy. She had a cadaverous face, hawk nose and frizzy hair. "We made candles," she said dourly. There they were on a central table, inside toilet-paper rolls, wicks held in place with chopsticks. Nancy nodded, but she was thinking about Charlie, his tongue in her ear. Now that was something to think about. She sat down in a small red plastic chair, the better to relive the charge. In fact, his tongue had been a bit big, cowlike even, but in retrospect the feeling it gave off was pointed, precise.

THE one and only time she and Charlie had made love was a year and ten months before. Boxing Day. The Christmas tree was in the corner, covered in chains of cranberries and popcorn. The house smelled like a forest. Shulamith went off to bed upstairs, but Nancy and Charlie stayed up late, drinking wine on the couch—and then that remarkable gesture: he reached out and put his hand on her heart. Why had he done that? It was what she always thought of, more than the sex, which wasn't, she had to admit, of the first waters. He wanted her to put her legs up, wrap them around his back. (Was this something women were supposed to be able to do easily? She did not have flexible hips, and supposed that Shulamith must.) Afterward, she said: Well, I'm glad we got that out of our system, knowing, without feeling it yet (the way you know things after a death), that everything would be different forever. What surprised her though, and interested her even, looking at it with a scientist's objectivity (a love scientist—ha ha), was how the memory acted. She could go for a morning not thinking about it, and then, bang, walking down the street or standing in a bank lineup, it would buckle in her gut, a bubble of life opening inside her—and with its own, electric attachments. It made her stop and groan, feeling him inside her in that way.

Since then they had said they would stop. And they had—because there wasn't really anything to stop. It was a one-off, a mistake. He had made that clear. But sometimes he came to the guest house and talked to her. They drank wine. And twice they ended up groping and touching (like snakes, like villains) while Shulamith worked late hammering out her press releases and responding to e-mails. They could see the light from her window through the trees.

"OKAY," Nancy said to Ramsey. "Let's go."

They walked out the door and through the driftwood gate of the school garden.

Ramsey stopped. "Where's the car?"

"I didn't bring it."

He looked as though he might run back to the schoolhouse, fling himself to the floor and scream.

Nancy said quickly, "I wonder which pocket holds the M&M's?" She made a bulge in one pocket with the bag, the other with her fist, and led the way around the schoolhouse to the trail. They started down it, through the trees, toward the shore, while he triumphantly guessed which pocket, then which hand, then which M&M. Ducking beneath an umbrella-shaped nest of cedar branches, they emerged onto the beach. It was the site of an old midden: a million crushed clamshells sparkled in the sun. The water was sharp blue. Together the two colours were like snow and sky, that clear and bright. The clouds had lifted and Nancy realized it was a beautiful day. She turned to Ramsey to say something about living in Paradise, but he was standing stock-still, sniffing the air like Nancy's old dog, Riley. Then he took hold of Nancy's jacket, moaned in terror and crumpled into a fetal position.

Nancy knelt, shocked.

"Ramsey? Yoo-hoo."

Nothing.

She turned over a rock and tiny black crabs scuttled out of the wetness. "Oh—crabs!"

She could feel Ramsey willing himself to stay rolled in his ball.

"I can't touch those things," she said. "They freak me out."

He sat up then and looked at her with the eyes of an angry king. "I'm telling Mum and Dad. You're not supposed to bring me down here."

"I bet these crabs bite."

Tears gathered, and rage grew in his body. Soon he would be howling, and she would need to pick him up and carry him back through the forest. But no: in the next second the fury passed through him. The entire drama was so *internal* she might have imagined it. He reached forward, plucked a crab from the watery divot left by the rock and held it in his cupped hands.

"They don't hurt, Auntie Nan," he said. "Hold out your hands."

He placed the crab in her hands, where it scuttled from palm to palm. "Ooh. Feels weird."

He squatted beside the hole, letting it go. Nancy moved to a snaky pile of kelp swarming with sand flies. She picked up a bulb and walked backward, letting the seaweed whip drag behind her. It was at least ten feet long, ending in a clutch of rubbery fingers. Ramsey ran and took it from her. He was back. He was himself.

You're amazing. (Charlie would whisper.)

How did you do it? (Shulamith.)

Firmness, she would tell them later. Firmness and M&M's.

They walked on, and the sun shone down on them. Ramsey whacked the bull kelp against the sand and the end leapt up.

A sandstone point marked the end of the beach. They would either have to clamber around the low-lying rim, past smooth caves in the rock, or cut across the top. Without a word Ramsey scrambled happily along a crack in the rock and onto the top.

It was like climbing onto the back of an animal. Even through the layers of running shoe and sock, the sandstone felt warm. Tidal pools glinted, their surfaces rippled by the wind. Below, on the flat, wet rocks, a seal spotted them and waddled to the water, where it became liquid—a flip of tail and it was gone.

Ramsey ran to the largest pool, seeming happy now, and Nancy felt a rush of gratitude and plea-sure—the same feeling she had had stepping onto the bright beach. She came and knelt beside Ramsey, and he unhooked his Spider-Man backpack and sat on it. One of his Velcro shoes had come undone, but he didn't seem to notice. The pool had a purple starfish in it and a clutch of anemones, tentacles outstretched.

Nancy said, "You look like your daddy."

No answer.

She dropped a mussel shell onto the centre of an anemone, where its stomach was. The tentacles closed in slow alarm. Behind them, in the forest, a breeze made its rounds in the trees, touching the tops of the cedars, receiving a shushing reply from the maples. It sounded like gods speaking. While Ramsey experimented, prodding the anemones with bits of shell, Nancy lay back on the sandstone and let the sun heat her face.

The wind was making her remember her grandmother's farm in the Ottawa Valley. She had been eight or nine, and she had stood in a field on a lichen-covered rock while the wind hit her fiercely, and spoke in her ears, and flapped at her clothing. It felt like it could have happened yesterday, she remembered the wind on her face so vividly, but she had been so different then, still master of her soul, the subject of her universe, leaping from the rock, trying to get picked up by the wind.

She sat up and stared at the bright water.

When had she stopped being her true self? When had she become this other Nancy, who made up lies and slept with her best friend's husband? She would reclaim herself, that was all. She would begin anew. When Charlie knocked at the guest house, she would tell him not to come in. She would change her life, move someplace completely new, like Moose Jaw. She had passed through once on the train. All around the small city, fields of yellow canola blazed in the sun. There would be bees everywhere. She would buy a new dog.

But there was more too.

She stood up now and began to pace, she was so excited. Here it was, as clear as the sun on her hands and face. She had an answer for Shulamith about why Ramsey had been afraid—not because nature was small, or suffering and diminished, but because it was so large still, and rustling, and thick, and alive. *We don't have to grieve for the planet.* This was what she would tell Shulamith triumphantly, as she led Ramsey across the driveway, through the front door. You don't have to grieve, my dear friend, or carry that immense weight a second longer, or worry that you're damaging Ramsey with your fears, because this thing, this spirit moving in the branches, it's bigger than any of us, and it simply can't be killed. It can't even be *understood.*

Nancy felt an easing in her chest, like the release of a barrel hoop, and in an impulse of love she squatted beside Ramsey and kissed the top of his head.

He flinched.

No. That was not what happened. (She thought about it many times after. Many times.) What happened was this: he did not look up from the pool, but he shivered. It was a cold gesture, as though he had been touched by a snake, and it seemed to emanate from his bones.

Nancy put her hand out again, experimentally, and stroked one of his long curls.

"Don't."

"Don't what?"

"Don't touch my head."

"Don't touch my head, *please.*"

He placed a mussel shell on the water's surface. They watched as it took on water.

"Why can't I touch your head?"

"You're not supposed to touch somebody unless they ask."

This was the stuff they learned at preschool, but knowing this did not make Nancy feel any better. She shifted her weight a fraction of an inch, and he looked up at her.

"Your shadow's in the way."

He was right again: her shadow had obscured the bottom of the pool. She stood and walked around the pool. "If someone as close to you as your auntie Nan kisses you, I think it's okay."

No answer.

"You don't want to be too strict about these things or people won't feel like kissing you at all."

She knelt on the other side of the pool. A current caused the shell to float past the anemone. Ramsey placed the shell within the tentacles. Frowzy legs groped, then began to tuck the shard into the flesh of its stomach. Would it hurt? At what point would the anemone realize its mistake?

Her voice sounded loud when she spoke again. "What do your parents say about me?"

There was a pause.

"I mean when I'm not there."

Ramsey found a twig in the tidal pool, and he used it to pry the shell out.

"Does your daddy say anything?"

"You can call him Charlie, not my daddy."

"What does he say?"

Nothing but concentration on his task. But she could feel him thinking. He reached in and grasped the shell, wetting his sleeve. In the commotion she almost missed his words. "He says you should get a life."

The sting of these words was so sharp it was almost interesting, like a wasp bite. Ramsey again placed the shell on the surface. "But," he said calmly, "you don't have to get a life—you have one already. Everyone does."

"Everyone does." She repeated the words to buy time. Nancy thought of how Ramsey had controlled his tantrum, folding it deep inside. Was he letting it out now, in this careful display of malice? Were children capable of this? She had no idea. She wasn't a parent. She didn't have a life.

"And what does your mother say?" she heard herself ask.

A pause, while he positioned the shell above the anemone, preparing to drop it.

"What does Shulamith say about me?"

"Nothing."

"What?" It hurt so much she wanted it twice. "What does she say?"

"She never says anything."

He pushed the shell and it floated down on the invisible current, where it disappeared into a patch of seaweed.

NANCY did not think of it as hiding. That would have been crazy and wrong, to hide on a child until he looked up and noticed his aloneness and screamed in terror, screamed her name and stood and—yes— there she would be, climbing up from below. It's nothing, see? It's nothing—just the wind moving the trees.

She inched her way, crabwise, across the rock, leaving him gazing into the pool like a small Narcissus. Then she stood and made her way down the sandstone until it formed a smooth shoulder near the forest's edge. She jumped down with a crunch into a driftwood nook on the beach, then undid her jeans and squatted. A hot stream poured onto the crushed shells. She shook and buttoned her jeans, then sat on the sandstone lip and lit a cigarette. A snake slipped between the rocks. The wind died and she heard him then.

AFTERWARD she was asked to relive it many times. First, in panic, as she yelled out to Shulamith across the gravel turnaround in front of the house. This was after beating her way up the trail, screaming his name, palms bleeding from her fall on the shell beach. *Is he here? Did he run home?* Then later, more slowly but still panicked, she told Charlie what she knew. Then, that afternoon, she went over it with the police. And eventually, slowly now, she described what had happened at the inquest.

Didn't you think a five-year-old might be in danger left on his own?

How long were you gone?

She had smoked a cigarette, but not all the way to the filter. That was her practice. She never smoked it all the way down.

She had peed.

At the inquest, Shulamith sat in the row ahead of her. Her hair was chopped short—she had gone at it with the kitchen scissors. Her head looked strangely small from the back, though she had (Nancy noticed this, over the high roaring of her own grief) the most beautiful neck Nancy had ever seen.

A minute. A single cigarette, not even smoked to the filter, butted on a rock, thrown onto the clamshells. Three minutes at most. The wind had been fierce and then it had died down and she had heard something.

A cry for help?

I think I heard a moan. Then I ran to him—I ran but he wasn't there. I ran home—

Shulamith's face in the turnaround. She had been pulling dead plants from a pot. She raised her gloved hand to her eyes and smiled. Then the shock as Nancy screamed that Ramsey was gone.

A wildlife expert said he believed that the animal, a female cougar, 145 pounds, had been tracking them since they reached the beach, or possibly even before, since reaching the trail that ran from the schoolhouse through the forest. In the time Nancy was absent (five minutes at most) it was possible that Ramsey glanced up, hearing a sound through the din of the wind, seeing something brown from the corner of his eye, hairs rising. He may have had time to stand as the thing moved toward him. He may have had time to run. If so, he exposed his neck. Puncture wounds showed beneath the sixth vertebra, severing the spinal column. Then the cougar dragged him over the ledge, into a hidden spot beneath the lip of sandstone.

This came out later.

For now Nancy stands beside the tidal pool, holding the Spider-Man backpack. A Velcro running shoe lies in the murky bed of seaweed. She is calling out his name but the wind tugs at her voice and sucks at the sleeves of her rain jacket.

Come out right now, Ramsey. I'm not kidding. Come out now.

You've done it, she screams at him, and past him at the wind moving everywhere, stealing her voice. *You win. Now come out. You've frightened me.*

IN DELPHI

1.

They had travelled for three days and arrived in Delphi, the centre of the ancient world.

"Where's the balalaika?" Nathan, Maya's husband, sat down across from her on the terrace of the Café Agora. "Where's the strumming of the lyre?" He bounced up again and crossed to the outdoor bar. Maya could hear him asking that the American music be turned down.

"That's better." Nathan, seated once again, unfolded his handkerchief and wiped his brow.

Maya turned away. *Help me*, she thought.

This trip was Maya's fiftieth-birthday present from Nathan: the fulfillment of a dream she'd had for years to come to Delphi, the seat of primordial wisdom, and pose a question at the temple of Apollo, just as travellers used to, from Persia or Lydia or Thebes. They came by foot or by chariot on the same winding route through the mountains

that Maya's bus had negotiated (God, what a trip—
her body was still rocking from the jolts and turns),
or they came by boat, blood-red sails bloating in the
wind, dolphins leaping in their wake.

The night before, Nathan had sent back his
moussaka because it wasn't hot enough. And now the
elevation seemed to be making him jumpy. Or perhaps it was the wind, blasting down from the heated
cliffs of Mount Parnassus. Maya turned to take in
the view below the terrace: olive orchards, a few sen-
tinel cypress trees casting an early shade, then the
slope turned raw and rocky for miles, foothills pleat-
ing a path leading to a stone hut, until, at last, the
entire, heated mountain flattened to a riverbed, the
famed Pleistos Valley, where five sacred wars had
been fought. Beyond that, at the tip of sight, Maya
caught a glint of azure, the Corinthian Sea.

Now Nathan leapt up to get the bill. No amount
of gesticulating seemed to have worked. The waiter
remained behind the counter, turned away from
them, washing beer glasses, which he lined up on
the counter upside down. Maya could see the line of
hair running from the waiter's bushy scalp down the
back of his neck, and she wished, almost violently,
that Nathan had a full head of hair.

The truth was, she thought, watching Nathan
receive his change, he was less than satisfactory

when taken out of his habitual milieu. He looked capable behind his teak desk, or on the balcony of their condo in the morning, freshly scrubbed, smelling of Saddle Soap, the line of men's natural cleansing products that Nathan distributed whole- sale. It was a smell of leather and profit, and it suited Nathan. But when you set him down in a for- eign locale, Thailand, for instance, or Greece, the top of his head gleamed like an egg in the extra sunlight.

Nathan sat down again. "Does the sand keep get- ting in your eyes?"

"I'm not sure. Something's getting in my eyes."

"It's sand."

Be still.

And he was, for a full thirty seconds, until: "Have you come up with your question yet?"

"Not quite yet."

"Today's the day."

"I know."

"Then we'll go now? To the temple?"

She shook her head. She wasn't ready yet, and after a moment Nathan offered the idea of visiting the museum first. Maya agreed, but still they did not move, and the wind banged a shutter closed and knocked over the sandwich board outside the café.

IN the hotel room, Nathan lay down on the bed and began to check his BlackBerry while Maya changed into her sandals. The hotel suite had two rooms, a sitting area that looked over the roof of the Café Agora and into the valley, and a bedroom facing a vine-covered courtyard. All night long they had heard tourists laughing on the road outside, Germans calling to one another. Now, in the morning, there was the heated huff of tour buses pulling up.

Maya stepped onto the balcony. Restaurants lined the cliffside with dark doors facing the street and terraces turned to the view. She could hear walkie-talkies blaring instructions for the tour guides. Petunias cascaded from the hotel balcony next to theirs, and Maya inhaled, closing her eyes. The scent, velvety and peppery, brought back summer nights at her parents' lake house in the Okanagan, the willow tree scuffing its leaves across the concrete patio, the clink of coffee cups as her parents entertained their friends. Then her mother calling to her to come out. *Maya wants to put on a show.* Dear God, her mother's voice, even in her head, was so affected. Terribly, dangerously affected.

Dance, darling.

The willow tree raked its long leaves across the cement. The stars shone, and you could hear swimmers going by, that was how close the lake was. You could hear waves lapping against the breakwater. Then Maya, age eighteen, ran through the doors painted bold Mexican purple and terracotta and leapt onto the terrace clad only in her mother's batiked scarves. She danced and spun, while the adults commented on her lithe figure, and her father said, *You send a girl to study dance at the Martha Graham academy and this is what you get back.* Jesus, what a showgirl she had been, even at eighteen.

One night as she danced, the knot at the nape of her neck slipped—she must have tied it very loosely—and her breasts spun free. It should have been humiliating, other teenage girls would have screamed and covered themselves, but Maya spun more fiercely, caught in a state of wonder at her own audacity, knowing she was desirable, spinning and spinning, her breasts jiggling in the moonlight. Her parents' friends applauded, and her mother shrieked with delight, while her father looked on darkly.

Maya went inside and closed the balcony doors with a clank.

"Are you ready?" This was Nathan, not looking up from his BlackBerry.

"Just about."

She slipped her new dress from its hanger. It was a muted plum shade, Grecian in design, with a pleated skirt. She had bought it for the trip, and she had been looking forward to wearing it, but now she wondered if it, too, was affected and showy. Would she look as though she had stepped off an urn? She remembered something nasty a lover once said to her, a friend of her father's. She stared at the folds of the fabric, hearing his voice in her head, feeling stung, though it was over thirty years ago. *You're young. And you can prance and dance and it doesn't much matter. But someday it will. You should learn the value of being authentic.* He had been bitter because she was breaking it off. They sat in a car with the rain pouring down, in an alleyway near the acting school she attended, and he told her, brightly and bitterly, as though it were an interesting fact, that she was the most pretentious person he had ever met.

She took the dress from the hanger and let it drop over her slim shoulders. She had to find a way to shake these voices—her mother's, Jim Tanenbaum's (that was the name of the old lover). In a few minutes they would walk to the temple ruins. Would it be hard to picture, from the remains, how once it had stood in a blaze of marble, Mediterranean gold displayed around it? In ancient days the oracle had been a woman called the Pythias. She sat on a tripod in the sanctum of the temple, over a chasm that belched fumes, giving answers about the future, but they were always in riddles. This was what had fascinated Maya as a child when her mother told her about the oracle, and fascinated her still: each riddle was simple on the surface, easy to interpret, but it carried a jagged hook—your own hubris, your pride, your desire to misinterpret.

The most famous example, one her mother had told her about years before (Maya lying on the floor in the kitchen, her mother drying and returning cutlery to the drawer with a swift abandoned clatter), was of King Croesus of Lydia. He wanted to attack Persia. He was hungry for rugs and Persian sweets, for lapis lazuli. So he sent an envoy to Delphi to ask what would happen. "Rest assured," said the oracle. "If you go to war you will destroy a great kingdom." So King Croesus waged war and lost everything to the Persians. It was only as he was led away in chains to be paraded through the streets that he remembered the oracle's prediction—and he grimaced, he had to, it was so clear now that the great kingdom had been his own sweet Lydia, Land of Horses.

So what would Maya ask? Why had she come all this way, by plane and boat, and last, by bus (an experiment with Greece's transit stations that entailed peeing in a tiled hole)? Why do all this if not to ask something important, something about turning fifty, an age she didn't like particularly, though probably nobody did. It was true she was still beautiful, with remarkable eyes and a slender body, a heart-shaped face and shapely feet. She had been in movies (only one soft porn), and a TV series that got cancelled, before she stopped all that and married Nathan. Now she practised Feldenkrais, and he paid the rent of her studio in False Creek, and she was still beautiful, that was what everyone said. But it made her ache to think how old she suddenly was.

Perhaps she groaned aloud, because Nathan appeared at the doorway of the bedroom. "Are you all right?"

"I'm fine."

"That's a pretty dress. It brings out the colour of your eyes."

He came and kissed her, first on the cheek and then on her eyelids. It was as though he knew she was confused and dissatisfied and wanted to lift these sensations from her with the dry kindness of his lips. But it did not work, and she turned away and buttoned her dress.

2.

It came with a great flapping. It came with the scent of the air before lightning. It came with magnificent certitude. It came in a flurry. It came, and it spoke to him. It whispered like a snake.

Nathan stood in the bathroom of the museum, clenching the edge of the sink. The polished concrete floor cast a glow through the soles of his feet and up his legs. He took a breath, but it was too late. Fingers twangled the top of his skull. He had the prescience to think, *At last, some Greek music,* before the Thing poured down his forehead and into his nose, carrying with it a scent of foreboding, of doom, and then, with something between a laugh and a groan, the Thing was gone.

Dear fucking God!

His eyes cleared. His head was framed in the mirror, his eyes furtive and alarmed. The message they held, the first message he could form, was: *for God's sake don't let Maya know.*

He had been sitting beside Maya, looking at a statue on a pedestal, when all at once his heart had thrashed. He made his way to the washroom, syrupy dots clouding his vision, then clung to the counter ledge.

Enough. Now Nathan took his pill case from his pants pocket, swallowed two sedatives and a blood thinner and closed the lid with a snap. When he returned to the atrium of the museum, Maya was still on the bench. He sat beside her, following her gaze to the stone statue. THE SPHINX OF NAXOS, the wall plaque said. It had stood outside the Delphic Temple for seven hundred years, a gift from the Island of Naxos. It had a lion's torso and legs, the wings of a griffin and the intense stare of a startled, angry woman. It was not at all like the Egyptian sphinx, with its mellow eyes and soft, square visage: this sphinx was taking things personally. It looked as though it could pick out, not just the travellers coming up the Sacred Way, but the dust at their feet, and the ants in that dust, and even the noise of the earthworms below. And it was ready to take offence at them all.

Nathan took a breath. Was this the thing he had seen at the tail end of his vision? He remembered scales, or the gaps between scales, and something flapping at him with huge, gristle-tinged wings.

Maya turned to him sharply. "Where have you been?"

He gestured to the sign for the men's bathroom.

She peered at him closely. "Are you taking your medication? Did you feel faint?"

"I'm fine."

She returned her grey-eyed gaze to the Sphinx. "Shall we?"

"I'm ready."

"Let's go, then."

IT was high blood pressure, Nathan told himself, and anxiety caused by travel. This was made worse now by Delphi itself, the town's precarious perch—a few sharp terraces, and then that raging valley below. And of course, Maya's moods didn't help either. She could get so caught up in her own unhappiness. One morning their apartment would be clean and vacuumed, crystals sparkling on the windowsill and then, with a clap of thunder, Maya would go under. Out came the white flour and sugar she kept hidden. Sometimes she used up half a pound of butter on sugar cookies, before lying on the couch, tender and swamped, watching reruns of *Buffy the Vampire Slayer*, or the entire Colin Firth *Pride and Prejudice* miniseries. She had (he had told her this, rubbing her belly) a remarkable nature. She was the cause of magic in his life. Though on this trip, he had to admit, his attention to her remarkable nature was taking a lot of effort.

Now Nathan walked toward the temple gates beside Maya, in her softly mauve, softly grey, softly pink dress with its pleats, and her sandals. They passed a group of middle-aged Greek men drinking espressos under a plane tree. The men stopped to watch Maya, appreciation on their faces. Strong cigarette smoke wafted toward Nathan and Maya. The leaves of the plane tree rustled.

Then one of the men muttered something to a man with grey hair next to him. Both looked hard at Maya, and then the younger man (not so much younger—in his forties) pushed back his chair and came toward them, stopping them beneath the tree. He was dark and stocky. He said some words in Greek before turning to his friends and laughing.

"We're English," Nathan said, which was ridiculous—they were Canadian. He meant they spoke English.

The man had mischief on his face. He said, "Your wife?"

Nathan nodded.

"She is like Greek goddess."

Maya smiled blinkingly at them. Then the men erupted in clapping. They clapped for her.

"Thank you," she murmured. "Thank you."

Nathan motioned to his watch, miming their tearing hurry to get to the temple. The bull-like man stepped aside, and Nathan and Maya carried on, into the hard sunshine beyond the tree. They heard an eruption of laughter as the man rejoined his group, and Nathan knew from the tone of their laughter, its darkness, that they had found Maya, or perhaps both of them, absurd.

He put his arm through Maya's and glanced at her face. She looked pale, her jaw clenched.

"Always the central attraction."

"Oh shut up, Nathan," she said. "I feel—" She reached into her bag for her glasses.

"What do you feel, darling?"

"Never mind, never mind." She put them on, thick things that covered her eyes. "Never mind," she said a third time.

And they carried on, toward a bank of laurel bushes that would shield the lower part of their bodies from the sun.

AT the entrance to the Sacred Way, Maya rested in the shade of a tree, while Nathan paid for their tickets. Calm temple dogs basked in the filtered sunshine. One with thick fur dislodged itself from the ground, shook itself and came to sniff her. Maya stroked its head, then Nathan joined her and they started together up the steps that led to the sanctuary.

The Sacred Way was eight feet wide, and paved in blocks of marble that had been broken here and there by ancient chariot wheels. Patches of dry grass poked through the breaks. Sun threw itself onto her neck and cicadas cried everywhere. A group of women in floral dresses came toward them, speaking something that sounded to Maya like Swedish. She stepped aside to let them pass.

"Maya—"

"Let's be silent for a while."

The marble of the road was so worn, the pieces

gleamed like slabs of skull. Foot-sized grooves had been driven into the stone and Maya noticed that her sandalled feet fit into them perfectly. The resinous scent of pine wafted from the mountain, along with the brash voices of tourists.

They reached the first curve in the path, and before them stood a small marble building with three columns. The Treasury of the Athenians. They admired it for a moment then carried on, up the second level, into the full, afternoon sun. Maya swatted a bug on her cheek and her hand came away bloody.

What does it mean to be fifty?

No—that wasn't it. But she was getting closer.

How should I live the rest of my life?

No. But closer still.

It had to do with life, and death, and mortality. She knew that. It had to do with an ancient ache in her bones. It had to do with dancing on the terrace, naked breasts bare, wanting to spin herself into another state, an ecstatic state, a "real" state, where she understood existence, but failing every time and instead preening and peacocking. The dark stare of her father. So much judgment. *You should learn the value of being authentic.*

I am authentic, she heard herself think, and yet all her life she had felt that there was, in fact, something artificial about her relationship to the world. There was a final level to descend to, an understanding to face. But what was it? She was closer now. She almost had it. With a final switchback of the path, the temple swung into view.

NATHAN had felt calmer all the way up the hill. With pleasure he had stood beside Maya, watching her take in the symmetry of the Athenian Treasury. Now, seeing the temple ruins in front of them, Nathan reached out, found Maya's forearm, and gripped it, while a small sigh of delight escaped his lips. Delight, yes, but awe too, at the sheer power of placement. My God, how the temple must have looked in ancient times, rounding that final corner. The startle factor. He could imagine the blast of marble, a priest bustling toward them, insisting they buy a goat to slaughter, the buzzing of voices beneath the parapets, the scream of the goat.

Maya looked at him. "Nathan, you've gone pink all over."

He wanted to say he was fine, but his tongue felt large and strangely stuck in his mouth.

"You're the colour of a lobster." She led him to a piece of toppled marble the size of a bale of hay. He sat, then wiped his forehead and palms with his handkerchief.

"Don't worry," he said. "I'm absolutely fine. I want you to go ask your question."

"You're soaked."

"Go. I'll cool off here."

She looked at him sharply.

"It's the altitude, that's all," Nathan said.

"You should be in the shade."

"The sun's at a slant. I'll be all right. I want you to consult the oracle."

SHADOWS lengthened from the columns of the temple—if indeed, Maya thought, you could call it a temple. The thing (Maya could not help smiling grimly to herself at the thought) was in ruins. A few cracked and mottled columns patched together and then re-erected by some patient archaeologists; a stone foundation and a surround of broken pillars piled about like logs. It was, like every single thing about being fifty, a disappointment, over which, with a masterful show of joie de vivre, it was up to Maya to throw a scrim of awe, and delight, and mystery. Her dance—and never had it seemed more clear to her—her lifelong dance had been to cover up the paucity of the world. This hit her with such force! It was a great, almost lustful surge of disappointment. It might have gathered in the four corners of the world and blown here, to this exact centre. And it was so terrible, so true and terrible, that her eyes filled with tears and she sat down on the marble bale in the sun, next to Nathan.

She had danced her heart out and it had all come to this: she was fifty, in a ridiculous costume-like dress, sitting on a rock with her husband, who had turned pink and was dressed head to foot in Tilley wear. And this place, this dreadful place, seemed to be saying, *Yes, go on. See it all as bleakly as you need to. This is what you came for. See the smoke-and-mirrors dance. See the bones underneath.*

It was then that her question came to her.

She stood quickly and gestured to a rocky outcropping that looked down on the temple ruins. "I'm going up there."

She hurried across the stones.

THE spangles cleared one by one from Nathan's eyes, like fading stars, and the excitement that had clutched his heart on seeing the temple began to lessen. He took a breath and then, to safeguard against another implosion, he took a pill, swallowing it dry.

The restorative magic. It gave him the courage to look across the skull-like stones at the pillars of the temple. And then he heard, at the back of his brain, the hammering of horses' hooves. The premonition he had kept at bay gathered at the corners of his brain. It flared; it flooded; a mineral taste filled his nostrils.

What he saw was this. Himself sitting, and Maya climbing onto the rocks above him. He wanted to call out to her, knowing he had done this before, and that the act of calling out would only push him closer to the centre of the déjà vu, clicking the shutter that caught doom in its lens.

But Maya was practically sprinting up the hill now, something new powering her joints. All the shadows were long, thrown down the valley from the temple pillars, and the shadow of every cypress tree was picked out shrewdly, as though to say, *There is life and there is death, and look how closely they lie together in this landscape.*

3.

That night, over dinner, when Nathan heard the question that Maya had asked the oracle, his first instinct was to tell her about his premonition, so that she could understand the danger. But it was too late, the question had been asked. And they were in fine moods, the olives so ripe and salty, full of oil, picked from the slopes beneath the restaurant. He let it pass. Perhaps he was wrong. He hoped he was wrong. Besides, everyone, he reasoned, had a path, and this was Maya's, to hurl her question at

the temple from the height of her stone pinnacle.
Wherever it led her she would have to go, and see
for herself.

And she would. Not too long after that mem-
orable dinner, because she was fifty years old, and
in fact so many parts of life, as yet unfelt and
unexplored, were hurtling toward her, whether she
wanted them to or not.

Nathan would gladly spare her all that. Just as he
would spare her her dance of bravery, her dance in
and out of doctors' offices: blood tests, CAT scans,
bone scans, PET scans. The tender way she reached
for his hand in the waiting room.

(*I want to really feel things.*
That wasn't exactly the question—but almost.)

Yes, the surprise would be his tenderness.
That would be something worth feeling, when the
time came. Worth feeling. Worth revealing. And
to recognize, in certain moments of calm (afternoon sunlight streaking the wobbly panes, lighting
the underside of the rhododendron leaves outside
her bedroom window), that she might not give it
up (meaning the cancer) if it meant giving up all
she would come to recognize about the wild, terse
nature of life, and about her marriage, and Nathan,

yes, especially Nathan—it always came back to him. The depth of his eyes, both mysterious (how could he love her so?) and real. He shocked her with his love; and the fact that it had been there all this time, beneath the surface, growing so steadily, astounded her.

(How can I feel this dance, this dance of life and death, at my core?)

WHEN Maya came down from the outcropping at last, Nathan looked carefully at her face. He worried that she might still be caught in the throes of dissatisfaction, their trip a failure, another disappointment; but no, she looked jubilant as she walked toward him, lit up in a way he rarely saw. She bit her lip as though she had done something naughty. And those eyes! Maya's bright, hungry eyes. Would he ever get enough of them?

"Done!" she sang out.

"Really?"

"Got it. Can we eat early? I'm starving."

"Me too."

"I want to eat that honey dessert. At the Café Agora."

"I want wine."

"I want olives."

"So you're happy with your question?"
"Ecstatic. I'll tell you over dinner."
"Then let's go, my darling."
And they did. Down the hill, together.

ACKNOWLEDGMENTS

Many people helped and supported me during the writing of this book. Caroline Adderson—critical reader extraordinaire—gave me a hundred insights and a sustaining friendship. This book owes so much to her. Eva Stachniak supported me at every stage, and I was fed by our talks about writing at Butler's Pantry on Roncesvalles. My mother, author Barbara Lambert, provided editorial guidance (and guidance in general). My thanks also to Betsy Warland, Zen wizard of the arts, and to my brother, John, for sending news of the Ex'n'Pop bar in Berlin. My thanks as well to the editors who published these stories in their magazines, providing incisive feedback.

My deep thanks to Patrick Crean for championing this book of stories, and for wise editorial guidance. I am grateful for the enthusiastic response Patrick gave this book at HarperCollins, and to the publishing team that saw it into print, with special thanks to Alan Jones, designer, and Allyson Latta, copy editor.

My thanks to John Metcalf for supporting my work in *Best Canadian Stories*, and personally, and for beautiful handwritten letters, which now hang on my wall. So many writers have felt John's influence and now so have I.

My agent, Anne McDermid, has been, from the beginning, a wonderful support and guide to the world of publishing. My thanks to her, and to Martha Magor Webb, Monica Pacheco and the other associates at Anne's agency.

I am particularly thankful for my partner, Bob Penner, for all he does that makes life lovely, in good times and hard times. I could not have written this book without him. Peter and Lucy, you are amazing—*and* you make life wonderful. Wendy and Karen—dear friends. What would I do without you? Colette and Huong—thanks for beaming your love across the country. I'd also like to thank my parents, Barbara and Douglas; my brothers, John and Jamie, and their families; my mother-in-law, Norma Penner; and my aunt, Lorna Schwenk.

Last, but most importantly, I would like to thank Madeline Hope, friend and musician, to whom this book is dedicated. Every day, in small ways and big, you teach me how to live. And your music lights my life.